SALLY CAMERON MYSTERIES - BOOK 2

Secrets of the Past
& MURDER

SHIRLEY GLOSTER

SECRETS OF THE PAST & MURDER
Copyright © 2018 by Shirley Gloster

All rights reserved. Neither this publication nor any part of this publication may be reproduced or transmitted in any form or by any means, electronic or mechanical, including photocopying, recording or any information storage and retrieval system, without permission in writing from the author.

Scripture taken from the New King James Version®. Copyright © 1982 by Thomas Nelson. Used by permission. All rights reserved.

This is a work of fiction. Names, characters, places and incidents either are the product of the author's imagination or are used fictitiously, and any resemblance to actual persons, living or dead, businesses, companies, events, or locales is entirely coincidental.

ISBN: 978-1-4866-1643-5

Word Alive Press
119 De Baets Street Winnipeg, MB R2J 3R9
www.wordalivepress.ca

Cataloguing in Publication information can be obtained from Library and Archives Canada.

*I dedicate this book to my very dear friend who encouraged my writing and passed away on November 30, 2017.
I will miss him.*

ACKNOWLEDGEMENTS

I want to especially thank my grandson, Dan Robertson, who is my right hand with a computer. I would be lost without his expertise. I also thank my family for their full support and help, and Suzanne, my marketing person.

I thank Sylvia St.Cyr of Word Alive Press and editor Evan Braun, for his patience, for putting up with me and my ideas on writing, and for making it make sense.

CHAPTER ONE

HELP!

Lisa Cameron paced the kitchen floor, having circled the room several times. Every step she took seemed to make the situation a little tenser. Murder was something that happened to other people and never knocked on one's own door.

Then again, this was only indirectly murder, wasn't it? No matter how many times she circled the room, she was unable to come up with any answers.

Murder was murder.

She knew no one would understand. Murder was all around her, no matter which way she turned. Until four weeks ago, she'd had everything a woman could want, and then some.

So how could this happen?

She refused to admit that she had been living with her eyes closed to reality in order to keep her life the way she wanted it. Just because she hadn't thought of something over all these years didn't mean it hadn't always been there—on the backburner, so to speak.

Lisa couldn't sleep, and could barely eat, so great was the tension. To suddenly learn all these secrets that had been hidden for so long, for them to be exposed… it was mind-boggling. Right or wrong, they would cause such pain for everyone concerned.

Who could ever believe she would find herself in such a predicament at this age? Her age made the situation all the more dreadful.

To tell the truth, she had no idea how she'd become involved in this mess. Her memory was normally good, so why had it forsaken her now when she needed it? No way was she going to accept her age as the problem. She was as bright as anyone half her age. There had to be another explanation for what was happening to her.

If she had killed those two girls, surely she would know it.

If only her mind would clear up so she could think. Her mind was so fuzzy, and she felt so tired. She had to concentrate and make herself remember that afternoon.

Years ago, she had married into a well-to-do family that valued its proud name. She and her husband Hilliard had never had children. Although there were a few nieces and nephews in the picture, she was only close to one of them; Sally had always been a dear child, coming to see her every summer for years.

Sally had grown into a beautiful and successful young woman. Lisa had been trying to get up enough nerve to call her to ask for help. But what to tell her? Murder wasn't easy to explain. This would devastate the whole family, never mind their precious name.

She had been trying to find a solution to this very serious situation without involving them. She and Hilliard had enough money to hire the best lawyer in the country, but he kept insisting that they hire his friend. Lisa was almost to that point of being thankful this country didn't have the death penalty.

If only she could remember what she had been doing in that apartment! But there was no use. Her mind was blank. She would love to blame all her trouble on Hilliard, to say that it was really his fault. Wasn't he somehow responsible?

She sighed as she thought how much she loved the prairies. The province of Saskatchewan was special, with its freezing cold winters, whiteout blizzards, and thick blankets of snow one could barely see through. Like all those who lived here, she loved this part of Canada. The weather grew on you. She wouldn't want to live anywhere else.

Every once in a while, she stopped her pacing to glance at the phone on the wall. She kept putting off the decision to make that important call to Sally in Toronto. She was so far away, yet it was only three hours by plane. If Sally turned her down, she would be heartbroken.

But Lisa couldn't do this alone. She needed help. Sooner or later, the whole world would know. What would she do then?

Lisa's very dear friend Marsha Livingston lived four apartments down the hall and two floors below. Marsha was an older lady who had lived a good life and now lived alone. Her husband had died after losing a lengthy battle with cancer five years ago. She and Marsha had lived close enough to each other for so long that they could come and go whenever they wanted. They often had afternoon tea and biscuits, visiting and laughing together.

Still, not even her best friend would be able to understand a problem like this.

Finally, out of real desperation, Lisa left her apartment and walked down the hall to the elevator. She quaked with every step she took, eventually stopping outside Marsha's door, unsure whether she had the courage to knock.

One thing seemed certain: Marsha would never call the police, and Lisa refused to turn herself in. Hilliard had said he would look after everything. The trouble was, she didn't think she could trust him either. How bad was that? They had been married almost fifty years!

Judge Hilliard Cameron had a great deal of power in this city. He was one of the good ole boys who had his nose in everything, and of course everyone knew it had been his money that bought him seats on so many committees.

Lisa had wealth of her own and loved all the charitable work she did. She was well known, and certainly her face was recognizable in prominent circles. She, too, belonged to many organizations and had seats on many boards. But that was where her similarities to her husband ended.

She knocked on her friend's door and waited minute.

"My goodness, is something wrong?" Marsha asked, opening the door. "You don't usually come down here at this time of night. Come in."

Marsha could see the worried look on Lisa's face. She walked ahead as Lisa followed her into the sitting room.

"Sit down, dear, and I'll put the kettle on."

In minutes, Marsha had tea brewing and cookies on a plate on the small round table. The two women sat in rocking chairs.

"I'm not sure where to start," Lisa said. "Just give me a couple of minutes."

Once Lisa had taken a few swallows of green tea, she began to share her serious problem. The word *murder* came up over and over.

Shock was truly written on Marsha's face.

"Lisa, my dear, dear friend, you must call your niece and ask for help," Marsha insisted. "First of all, there's no way you killed those prostitutes. Had it been me, I might have done something like that. You? Well, being honest, you're not the type."

"Yes, you're right. But Marsha, I keep chickening out. How would I explain something like this to my niece? Sally and I are close, but this is too personal. Too private. I'd be so embarrassed." Lisa shook her head back and forth. "I've been trying to think of answers and it's impossible. Sally would help me if there were any way do it, but it's really not that simple. What am I to do about my husband? And what about Sally's father, my husband's brother? Worse, they're identical twins, two peas in a pod. If you were in Sally's place, who would you believe?"

Marsha looked at her friend and saw the suffering on her face. "Like I said, there's no way you killed them. So to heck with it and call the girl. I honestly don't see what choice you have."

"Truth is so important to Sally. Right from the beginning of her career, she needed to make her own decisions in a man's world." Lisa looked down at the slippers on her feet. "And there's another problem where Sally is concerned. In all these years, she's never fallen in love. Six months ago, to my surprise, she called and told me about a young man she met. She went on talking about this guy, Mark, for a good hour. Now she has his grandmother's beautiful diamond ring on her left hand! They haven't set a wedding date, but I imagine it'll be soon. And just to show you what I'm up against, would you believe that her fiancé is none other than an inspector in the Toronto Police Department? So you know where he must stand. That's why I'm frightened to call Sally. Her young man catches killers and puts them away. That's his job."

"Oh dear, what will we ever do?" Marsha's hand flew to mouth. "But he's from down east. He has nothing to do with the law here." She managed a laugh. "See what I mean? We're not asking your niece to practice law in Saskatchewan. We're strictly asking her for help or advice."

Their rocking chairs moved with ease, their thoughts running with each back and forth motion.

"Please call her," Marsha said after a while. "I can't help you with this." Then she had another thought. "How close is Sally to her father? Those two men are so similar. Have you considered they may both have kept the same secrets all these years? If that's the case, maybe your niece will be on your side."

"Oh my. I never thought of that. When she came here for her last holiday, she spent her time with me. She didn't seem to care for Hilliard, and I didn't mind." She smiled for the first time that night. "Marsha, you're such a special friend. I do believe I can face anything with your support. Why is it that when we're older no one really seems to care what happens to us?"

"My dear, old age is no fun. We're too easily forgotten." Marsha handed her the phone. "You obviously have faith in the girl, so what are you waiting for? Call Sally. Do it right now."

Lisa looked at the thing in her hand like it might explode.

"Your husband is having one of his nights out, I suppose," Marsha said. "You need to talk to someone before the police show up to arrest you!"

She held the phone, still weighing her decision.

"All right, I'll do it," she decided.

With a manicured pink fingernail, she punched in her niece's phone number and waited for it to ring. She had no idea what she was going to say, but she would play it by ear.

It's late there, with the time change, she thought, listing to the ringing phone. She had the greatest urge to hang up before Sally answered.

Lisa wasn't normally such a weakling, but tonight she was afraid for her life. If she didn't get help, she would spend the rest of her life in a home for the mentally ill.

Or prison.

* * *

Sally sat straight in her office chair, eyes on the computer screen. Her back ached, so she stretched her arms over her head and breathed deeply. The exercise brought some relief to her shoulders from bending over the keyboard.

CHAPTER ONE: HELP!

The phone rang and she reached automatically to take the call, not even thinking about leaving it for the answering machine.

"Hi, Sally here," she said into the receiver, overtired.

"Sally dear, it's Aunt Lisa. I'm sorry for the late call. How are you tonight?"

"Wha–a–at?" she stammered. Her voice brightened. "What a surprise! I'm fine. What a nice thing to hear your voice."

Sally thought she should have asked why her aunt would be calling so late at night.

"We're doing quite well, dear. I was just wondering when you might be coming out for a visit? You haven't been out since last Thanksgiving, and that's almost nine months ago. I read about your latest case in the papers. You did a wonderful job. You must be exhausted. I hope that new boyfriend isn't stopping you from coming to see me."

She paused, so tired. Was that the only reason for the call? Considering the time, this was ridiculous.

"Of course not, Aunt Lisa," she said politely. "You know there's nothing I would like better."

In the background, Sally heard a woman's voice say "Lisa, tell her and get on with it."

"I will, dear," her aunt said to the voice. Then she spoke to Sally again. "Sally, I know you're busy. I'm calling because I really need your help. You know all about blackmail and murder, right? I really am desperate. I'm in trouble."

Sally wondered if she was hearing right. "What in the world are you talking about? What does blackmail or murder have to do with you?"

This isn't making sense, Sally thought. *I must be too tired to understand. I can't have heard her right.*

"I don't understand, Aunt Lisa. "Who are we talking about?"

"Me! I know it sounds weird, Sally. I was just going to ask your advice, but now I realize that I need you to come out here. It's urgent, dear. I'll explain all about the trouble I'm in when you come. I don't even know how it happened. Sally, you're the only one who can help me. I fear they're going to arrest me on murder charges."

"Aunt Lisa, you're frightening me." Suddenly, Sally was wide awake. "What in the world are you talking about?"

Her mind was doing all sorts of flips trying to read the voice and understand the anxiety coming over the telephone line. She must be missing something?

"Did you kill Uncle Hilliard?" After she said it, the words sounded awful.

"No, my dear." She chuckled. "Please, Sally, let me know when you're arriving and I'll meet you. And come alone. I'll meet your young man some other time—that is, if I live that long."

Sally looked down at the receiver in her hand. The voice was gone; her aunt had just hung up.

This was ridiculous. If she lived that long? Sally was much too busy for this nonsense.

Immediately, she punched in her aunt's phone number. She waited and waited, but her aunt didn't answer her phone. She hung up, waited a few minutes, and then tried again.

Nothing. Perhaps her aunt had been calling from someone else's number.

What was she to do now? Wait until morning? Maybe it would make more sense then. Maybe she should call her father and ask about what was going on. But she really didn't want to call her father unless it was absolutely necessary.

She put the receiver back and pushed away from her desk. She was too busy to head to Regina on short notice, although she loved her aunt dearly. She loved travelling out west! If only she wasn't so busy.

Sally pulled the phone back to her ear and dialled another number. No one answered.

Maybe her father had gone to bed.

Just as she was about to hang up, she heard the receiver lift.

"Hello, Cameron residence," her dad answered.

"Dad, did I get you out of bed?"

"No, I was working actually. I have a sentencing coming down tomorrow, and it's going to be a hard one. To what do I owe this call in the middle of the night? I know it isn't because you miss me."

Sally ignored that last remark. She wasn't going to get into that now. He always had a sob story for her.

"I just received a call from Aunt Lisa, and it was a bit on the peculiar side. She wants me to come out for a visit. I was wondering, have you talked with Uncle Hill lately? Is everything all right out there?"

"Yes, of course I have. I talk to him once a week." Her dad paused. "I'm not surprised you heard from Lisa. Hill seems quite concerned about her. He seems to think she's going quite batty, causing all kinds of trouble in her old age. He's even considering putting her in some kind of mental home. I should have mentioned it, but I didn't want to worry you."

Hill should keep a closer eye on his wife, he thought. *He promised Lisa wouldn't call Sally. We don't need Sally anywhere near this mess.*

"I know how close you are to her, but reason sometimes gets lost when the mind goes," he said. "I would just ignore the call."

"You mean she's going senile?" Sally asked.

"According to Hill, she imagines all sorts of ridiculous things and talks about killing people who are her enemies. You don't have to worry about it. She's in good hands."

"I don't like the sound of this at all. Has he brought her to see a doctor?"

"Yes, he has. I would suggest that you leave her to your uncle and let him cope with her. I've been through the same with your mother. Not senility, but her heart attack was no easy thing to deal with. Who knows? One day, you may face a similar thing with me. If you're smart, you'll pass me on to one of your brothers."

That'll be the day, she thought.

"Okay, I won't bother you any longer," Sally said. "I'm exhausted and going to bed. I'll let you know if I decide to go."

"Oh Sally, that would be a mistake and a waste of your time. We shouldn't interfere. It's none of our business. Your uncle is more than capable of looking after his wife. Please, Sally, just leave this alone." He coughed into the phone. "By the way, how's Mark? You still haven't set a date. Why don't you let the poor fish off the line? Like it or not, you'll always be my girl."

He was asking for it, but she wouldn't take the bait.

"Dad, it's too late for this. I'll talk to you tomorrow night."

Count to ten, she thought. *You're the one who called him, remember?*

"Good night, Dad."

She still had one more call to make—to Mark. She quickly dialled and waited for an answer. When he finally did, it took her a few minutes to explain the call from her aunt. She had hoped Mark might provide some clarity, but she ended up still not knowing what to do. She decided to call him back in the morning.

She didn't like her father's attitude—and as for her uncle, he should have been standing by Aunt Lisa's side. She needed to sleep on this and make a decision in the morning when her head was clearer.

Half an hour later, she said her prayers and got into bed. She tossed and turned until sleep finally won out.

CHAPTER TWO
A SURPRISING TRIP

Sally opened her eyes as the alarm clock chimed. She looked at the windows, to assure herself that it really was morning. The sun was shining at least, making for a nice day.

Why was it that when everything was going so smoothly, something always came along to upset the apple cart? That phone call last night had been so out of the blue. It had completely thrown her. This nonsense with Aunt Lisa had her really worried. All the talk about blackmail and murder sounded ridiculous!

Her aunt was a saint. Dad might be right. Maybe she did have that dreaded dementia, or Alzheimer's, and if so it wasn't her fault. But she would also be surprised if that turned out to be true, since her Aunt Lisa had always been so full of life. She'd never had any trouble with her memory that Sally knew of. She had been fine nine months ago when Sally had last visited.

No way could she just abandon her aunt when she needed help.

She made her way from her bed and had a quick shower, brushing her teeth. Next, she pulled her damask travel bag out from under the bed and opened it, laying it atop the blanket. Wrapped in a thick, luscious bath towel, she picked up her phone and punched in a number. Only a few minutes later she had a seat on that morning's flight to Regina.

Then she made another call.

"Trotter here," her boyfriend answered.

"Good morning, Trotter," she said with a soft purring sound.

"Don't tell me, I already know," Mark said. "You're going to Regina, aren't you? Sally, you and I have someone watching over us. This couldn't work out better. I just talked to my boss and I'll be undercover for the next six to seven days. But you'll be too busy to miss me or worry about me. I'll be fine."

"Okay." She hesitated slightly. "Mark, you be careful. I know I'm not supposed to worry, but I do, just a tiny bit."

Sally knew he was just doing the job he loved. In truthfulness, though, it was almost more than she could take. She hated the undercover stuff. She also knew it was his life and his decision. No way would she ever try to change this man. She wouldn't want to.

"Only a tiny bit? That's not enough." He laughed. "I'll be fine. Anyway, you know how much this means to me. I'll see you when you get back. I love you. Have fun."

* * *

Several hours later, Sally was sitting in the back seat of a taxi as it left the Regina airport. It was early on a Thursday morning in the middle of August. She watched out the window as the cab moved along familiar streets. She could tell that this prairie city had been growing by leaps and bounds since her previous visit.

Sally thought the sun shone over this province more days than anywhere else in Canada. That was an added bonus, for sure. The sky seemed to have no boundaries. It had a gloriously bright, brilliantly blue look, proclaiming its power. Even now, her gaze travelled as far as it could out towards the horizon.

CHAPTER TWO: A SURPRISING TRIP

"Will you pull over at the nearest place where I can buy a newspaper?" she asked, leaning over the seat toward the cabby. Almost as soon as she asked, she spotted a corner newspaper stand. "There! Can you get me all the latest editions?" She handed him a ten-dollar bill.

"Sure, ma'am!" He pulled the cab over to the curb for a quick stop. He was out and back in seconds, then turned and handed the newspapers to Sally along with her change. "Regina's a busy place. There's always something doing here."

She smiled. "Thanks."

Within seconds, they were on their way again. Sally pocketed the change, sat back, and stared at the top's paper headline.

Indescribable shock passed through her as she dropped it back on the seat, as if it were boiling hot. She chose another paper, then another, and finally the last one. Every headline said the same thing, proclaiming the impossible.

She knew she had gasped. Now she just sat there, numb with shock.

"I wonder if you can do me another favour?" she said. "I need some time before I get to the address I gave you. Would you mind going to Wascana Park? I'll just be an extra few minutes. I'll pay for the added time."

"Sure, ma'am! You do know that it's in the opposite direction from the address you gave me, and it'll cost you a bundle."

"That's all right. I really need to compose myself. I didn't expect the headlines in today's papers. Please, just take your time."

So her aunt had been arrested and charged in the killing of two street girls. Positively ridiculous!

"Okay. You're the boss, lady!"

Why did I have to pick this one up today? he thought to himself. *At least she looks like she has money. Hopefully she's not a high-priced hooker. Maybe she's a good tipper!*

13

"You're sure about this, lady?" he asked again.

"Yes, I am."

Ignoring the driver, Sally settled back in her seat. *My God, what is going on? Now I know why you've brought me here. There has to be some dreadful mistake. But then, you know that already. Lord, help me to understand what I can do for Aunt Lisa.*

She opened the newspaper again and studied the headline: JUDGE'S WIFE CHARGED WITH MURDER. Her head spun and she felt cold all over. Her eyes glanced down to the rest of the story. Two prostitutes found dead. Judge Cameron's wife charged in the death of two street girls. She had admitted to the charges.

She closed her eyes for a minute, trying to relax. Then she opened them again and started to read:

> Lisa Cameron has confessed to killing the girls out of contempt for their corrupt lifestyle having led her husband into an affair with them.
>
> "They were the ruination of good family men, and men of the city," said Cameron, who claims to have walked into their apartment and shot them both.

In spite of everything, Sally had to smile at that word—*ruination*. It did sound like a word her aunt would use. Still, it was preposterous to accuse her of murder. Her uncle having an affair? That alone was ridiculous. He was too proud of his name to take such a chance. Then again, sometimes men didn't think they would ever get caught.

Finally, when she was thinking straight again, she looked up and found that they were driving along a road next to the river.

"This is such a beautiful place, this park," she mused aloud. "It's so peaceful. Will you stop a minute? Keep the meter running.

CHAPTER TWO: A SURPRISING TRIP

I just want to walk a few minutes. I have a lot on my mind, and I won't be long. I don't want you to lose any money."

"You're coming back, lady?" he asked, not sure what she was up to. She was a rather strange woman. He didn't want to get stuck with the fare.

"Please, don't leave me here. I do need to go to that address I gave you." Sally dropped her purse on the front seat of the cab, then left the car and walked over grass toward a path.

Twenty minutes later, she was back facing a worried-looking taxi driver. His expression made her laugh, despite all of her troubles. She knew he had followed her at a distance, maybe to make sure she didn't jump into the river or something.

"Please, carry on to the address I gave you," she said as she climbed back inside. "You have no idea how much I appreciate your honesty and watching me while I walked, but I'm tough and can look after myself."

"Yes, ma'am. You know, this ride is going to cost you a bundle." He reached over the seat and handed back her purse. "I never even looked inside."

"Thanks," she said, but she wasn't so sure. Had he connected her to the Cameron name? "Don't worry, I have the money."

He was glad the purse was back in her hand. That had been a scary few minutes. She might have had him arrested for taking her wallet! He looked at her face through his mirror, thinking she was a very strange woman indeed. He could have had three tips by now.

As the cab started driving back, closer and closer to her aunt and uncle's apartment, shockwaves moved through her body. Her mind vibrated with emotion, tossing her being in all different directions. One thing seemed sure: her aunt was going to need a good lawyer.

"Are you okay, lady?" The cab had stopped. "You look awful. You're not going to pass out on me, are you? This is the address you gave me. Do you need some help?"

"I'm sorry. My mind was somewhere else. I'm fine, thanks. How much do I owe you?"

He told her and she didn't seem shocked.

"Thanks, I appreciate your help," she said, handing him more than enough. "Please keep the change. I know you would have made it on other passengers in the time I took. But this was important to me."

He looked at her with an apologetic expression. "I can't do that, ma'am. It seems to me you have enough trouble ahead of you. You had better keep your money."

"I'm fine, believe me. I appreciate your patience."

Sally opened the door and had one foot out when she noticed three or four people standing around the front entrance to the large condo building. No doubt these were reporters. Now what was she going to do?

It was too late to turn back, but maybe no one would recognize her. She had to go into that building regardless. She made her way from the cab, her bag in tow and the papers under her arm, walking straight ahead, hoping that she looked like she lived there.

She opened the heavy glass door, pushing as it swung in. She was so thankful to see a security guard inside, even though he looked big and ugly. He obviously wasn't going to allow the reporters in. On the other hand, he might also stop her from going upstairs.

"Do you live here, miss?" The large uniformed man came to stand right in front of her, so she couldn't move one way or the other. He was too big to argue with.

She looked right at him. "No."

"Nobody's allowed in unless they live here. I'll need to see your key as identification."

"I'm Judge Cameron's niece," she said, crossing her fingers behind her back. "I have my driver's licence and my business card with me, if that will help. I'm Mrs. Cameron's lawyer as well."

Sally struggled with her little purse to retrieve her identification. She finally found what she was looking for and showed him her driver's licence.

"I'm here to help," she said. "I hope."

"You had better be who you say you are." The guard looked her up and down, dubiously. "Everyone in this building is very fond of the Camerons and we don't want them harassed."

Cameron. That name's given me nothing but trouble, she thought. *Well, maybe one of these days I'll be changing it to Trotter.*

As he let her by, she realized that he had only been doing his job.

She rode the elevator up, then started down the hall, passing a few doors and stopping in front of a door with a lovely wreath hanging on it. It had beautiful salmon flowers and a tiny blue bird nestled in the foliage. She thought her aunt had probably made the wreath.

The door also had a small brass knocker designed to look like the scales of justice. Sally stared at it for a few minutes. Sometimes those scales didn't balance just right. This had better not be one of those times.

She knew she couldn't stand here the rest of the day, so she lifted the knocker and wrapped two times.

A middle-aged woman opened the door and grabbed Sally, hugging and clasping her in her bosom.

Sally decided that the security guard must have called up ahead of her. Anna was a very nice woman and had been part of the establishment for as long as Sally could remember. Anna had completely supported her aunt over the years.

"Oh Sally, we need you so badly," Anna said with her slight old English accent. "You have no idea how I was hoping you would get here. Your poor uncle is beside himself with worry. I've had to call the doctor in twice. It's terrible, just terrible." She let out a moan. "Poor Lisa, she must be having a terrible time in jail with all those awful criminals. They locked her up! And the awful things people are saying. It's unbelievable!"

Sally didn't move, as Anna was holding onto her like a life preserver. She couldn't imagine what her aunt and uncle would ever do without Anna. She was so possessive of them. She had been their live-in housekeeper for years.

Finally, Anna let her out of her grasp, looking at the papers under Sally's arm.

"This is all a dreadful shock to me, too," Sally said. "You must hold on. My aunt and uncle need your strength. Did you say my aunt is in jail?"

"Yes. Because she's being charged with first-degree murder, there can be no bail. Poor Lisa is locked up with all those bad people. Sally, it's more awful than anything you can ever imagine. What are we going to do?"

"Right at this moment, I hardly know what to do myself. How about getting me a coffee? After I've talked to my uncle, you can fill me in on what's happened." Sally stepped inside and looked around. "Where is he, Anna?"

"He's in his den, dear," she said very softly. "He's no good to anyone right now. I think you should come and sit with me for a while and have that cup of coffee. By then, he may be feeling better."

Sally hoped her mouth didn't fall open. What in the world did Anna mean by that?

"I have to talk to my uncle," Sally insisted. "Time is ticking and I presume Aunt Lisa is locked up in the city jail."

CHAPTER TWO: A SURPRISING TRIP

Not waiting for an answer from Anna, Sally walked away, noting the anxious look on her face.

"Miss Sally, you really need to wait awhile," Anna said, following after her. "No, no, Miss Sally, please let him be. He's not able to talk to you now. He's upset. He's not well. No, no! Please, it's hard to see him like this."

Sally ignored her, not liking what she saw in the woman's expression.

She tapped on the closed door of her uncle's den, but there was no answer. She did it again, a little louder, hurting her knuckles.

She opened the door when she received no answer again.

"Uncle Hill, its Sally. Are you all right?"

Her first look at the den told the whole story, not to mention the smell. Standing in the doorway, Sally couldn't believe her eyes. Her ever so perfect uncle was slumped over his desk, his mouth open with drool trickling onto his half-open shirt. His silk tie lay on the floor in a cast-off heap. She grimaced.

It was obvious that he was completely sloshed. Bottles of booze were everywhere, on top of his desk and all over the floor. A few were tipped over, their contents dripping onto the expensive carpet. There was even an open bottle of pills!

She held her nose and shook her head, not believing what she was seeing. This explained what Anna had been worried about. Not only that, but she could practically feel Anna standing right behind her, staring over her shoulder.

Anger ran through Sally. She dared not turn to look at the housekeeper, who had been trying to hide her uncle's dirty secret—that he had turned to whiskey to solve his problems.

When Sally did finally turn, Anna was gone. Who could blame her? For all Sally's anger, she was only the hired help.

Sally left the den and found Anna in the kitchen.

"Anna, I in no way approve of my uncle's conduct," Sally said. "I don't understand it, when he's such a strong man. Anyway, it appears he won't be available at the moment to help anyone, so I need you to be calm. I know you can do what I ask."

Now, if I can just follow the same advice, we'll have it made, she thought to herself.

Anna nodded. "Yes, dear."

"When was the last time the doctor was here? My uncle had a pill bottle beside him on the desk."

"I called him right after the police left with your aunt. That was in the early hours of the morning, before the sun came up. Then I called him again around ten o'clock, after he woke up. The judge hasn't been feeling well all week. I don't ask questions, you understand. It's not my business."

"Did the doctor come right here to the apartment?" Sally asked.

"Yes, ma'am. He's been our doctor for years and years."

"You're lucky. They don't make house calls anymore where I come from, never mind in the middle of the night. Has he been drinking ever since then?"

Anna hesitated. "He didn't start to drink until after the doctor left the last time. You can't blame him for that. He's been through more than any soul should have to bear. Just imagine, his wife being arrested! If you ask me, the police need to be out looking for the real killer, not arresting old women."

"Anna, I need to know the facts, and personal feelings have to be put aside for a bit. You're here all the time and you know these two people better than anyone. Now, is my uncle involved in any drugs or prostitution?"

"Of course he is, dear. What judge doesn't have to deal with those kinds of things? Those girls who were killed, though, they were nothing but cheap tarts. They were into drugs. That's why they died!"

CHAPTER TWO: A SURPRISING TRIP

"Anna, I know all about street girls and drugs. What I don't understand is how this has anything to do with my aunt and uncle."

"It doesn't. That's what I'm trying to tell you."

"Then how did Aunt Lisa get mixed up with those girls? How in the world could she be blamed for killing them?"

"I really don't know, dear. She was always helping the poor people."

Sally realized right then and there that she wasn't going to find out anything here. If she kept going like this, she would end up screaming at the housekeeper.

"Anna, did my uncle's secretary ever come here to the apartment?"

"Oh no, ma'am, never. You mustn't believe what the papers say about your uncle. It's not true. Your uncle is one of the finest men God ever made. It's all lies, every bit of it."

Sally left the apartment.

Out in the hall, the doors to the elevator opened and she once again stepped into the dreadful machine. She stood to the side, alone, as the elevator rode down. She hated to admit how quick this was compared to taking the stairs.

There was so much she didn't know about what had happened. What had led the police to charge her aunt with murder? Well, she was going to find out.

But she had a strange feeling in the pit of her stomach that they were going to give her the run-around.

CHAPTER THREE

AT THE COURTHOUSE

Sally left the building intent on seeing her aunt and talking to her. But she had to take this one day at a time—one hour at a time, actually.

She arrived at the city courthouse and made her way inside where she was greeted by a receptionist. Crossing her fingers again, she explained that she was Lisa Cameron's attorney. She was fairly sure that was the only way she would get to talk to her.

After proving her identity, the receptionist let her in and gave her directions. Sally walked to where she had been told to go and found herself standing in front of a uniformed policeman sitting in a straight-backed chair. He was reading a paperback. Behind him was a plain, unmarked wooden door with a lock on it.

This didn't surprise her, although the chair looked too uncomfortable to casually read a book on.

"Can I help you?" the policeman asked.

Sally thought he must have been warned she was coming. "Yes, I'm sure you can. I'm Sally Cameron and I'm here to see my aunt. If I followed the directions right, I must be in the right place."

He seemed like an even larger man when he stood up. "Sure, no problem, Ms. Cameron." He smiled. "She's a dear old lady. Everybody likes her."

"Thanks. I appreciate that."

Sally walked in through the open door, which closed heavily behind her. She oriented herself for a moment, then noticed her aunt sitting in a bright yellow stuffed chair. This certainly wasn't like any cell she'd ever seen. It had a large window, rather high up the wall, and it was barred. The room was small, though clean and comfortable, with a single bed, a chest of drawers, a small round table, and a chair. Sally spied a washroom through an open door.

She was surprised her aunt didn't look up when she came into the room. She walked closer.

"Hello, Aunt Lisa." She bent and kissed her aunt's cheek.

Lisa didn't react, and a wave of panic passed Sally's mind. Just when she was about to scream for help, Sally realized that her aunt must just be ignoring her. How strange!

"Aunt Lisa, you called me and I came. I'm so glad you called. I'm just sorry I didn't get here sooner."

"I'm told this room is special, for VIPs," Lisa said, finally lifting her head. "However, there's one little catch: it has a locked door. Judith says if my husband weren't a judge, I wouldn't be in here. I would be in the city jail, in a dirty cell. So I'm supposed to be thankful for that."

"Who's Judith?" Sally asked, leaning in so that their faces were just inches apart.

"The crown attorney." Lisa grazed Sally's cheek endearingly. "Life is strange when you're supposed to be thankful for being in jail, wouldn't you say? Helping people one day and then locked up the next. How can one explain that?"

"I don't know, Aunt Lisa. You're right, it sure is strange." She looked around and didn't find any other seats except for the one tucked under the round table. She walked over and carried it back to where her aunt was sitting. She took Lisa's slender hands in her own. "I don't understand what's going on. I hoped, once I talked to you, that you could clear up the situation."

Sally looked down at her aunt's hands, trying not to think about the murder charges.

Lisa now smiled. There was a sparkle in her eyes as mischief danced on her face. "Sally, I'm glad you came." She paused, her face turning serious again. "I know it's going to be difficult for you to understand why I killed those girls, but our streets are overrun with prostitutes taking advantage of young men."

Sally looked at her aunt, aghast. She was sure her mouth must have fallen wide open. First, there was no way her aunt had killed anyone—but she had admitted it! The next thing that came to her mind was a question: was the room bugged? She hoped not. This statement of guilt sure wouldn't help.

"I have to say, you surprise me," Sally said. "You're different than when I usually come to visit."

"Well, the circumstances are different."

"Aunt Lisa, I remember one year, when the weather was unusually cold, you went out and bought eighty brand-new warm coats. Then you went down to poorer parts of the city and gave them to away to girls who were prostitutes. I also remember when you helped serve hot Christmas dinners at a local hall for homeless girls. You footed the bill for that. I don't think I could count on both hands the girls you've helped get off the streets. So you can see why this story doesn't work for me." Sally sighed. "I could go on, but what you're saying just doesn't make a lot of sense. Have you hired a lawyer to defend you against these charges?"

"You don't understand, my dear. A lawyer is the last thing I need." She smiled. "Sometimes our lives are changed by things we have no control over, and the next thing we know we're faced with tough decisions. Sometimes you just do what you must. In this case, a lawyer won't help. A lot has happened since that phone call. I shouldn't have called you, mixing you up in my troubles. I'm not sure where to start explaining what's happened, and I'm not sure I want to. My mind goes hazy whenever I try to think. You must understand that I've decided to plead guilty to killing those dreadful girls."

"Really? But we both know you didn't do it."

"Hill told Judith that one of his lawyer friends will look after me. His name is Ben." Lisa sighed. "Hill doesn't understand that I don't want his lawyer. I never cared for Ben very much, and he isn't even a defence attorney. Or maybe it's just a personality thing. He never did business with me. It was always your uncle."

Lisa shifted in the yellow chair that she'd been sitting in too long. Her back ached a little bit as she raised her head, catching Sally's eye. If only she could remember what had really happened. But she couldn't.

"The first thing I want you to do is stop listening to Judith and the judge," Sally said. "No more taking their advice, no matter what they say. Please, only do what I suggest until I can find someone to help us. Do we have a deal, Aunt Lisa?"

"Whatever you like. It really doesn't matter. You see, Sally, my future is settled. If you talk to Judith and listen to what she says, you'll see that it's settled. Watch her very carefully. She has a great deal of power in this city." Lisa yawned. "If you don't mind, I'm tired and tomorrow will give me a chance to put my thoughts in order."

There was something very odd going on here, Sally realized. Why couldn't she put her finger on it? Then, as she concentrated on her aunt's eyes, she knew what the problem was. There hadn't been any stroke or illness. Medication had to be the culprit. Her aunt was a little bit doped up.

Now that she knew what was happening, she was determined to do something about it.

"Sally, are you staying with Hill?" Lisa asked.

"I'll have dinner with him tonight. Anna is doing some of her special baking. She's very worried about you, too."

"That's nice of her, dear."

"I may just stay at a hotel while I'm in town. Uncle Hill has so much on his mind. I don't want to be a bother."

"That's probably a good decision."

Sally decided there was only one way to deal with this situation. She grabbed a piece of paper out of her purse and scribbled a few lines on it with a pen.

"Aunt Lisa, I need you to sign this statement. It says I am to be your lawyer, and that I'm working for you, not Uncle Hill." She handed the paper to Lisa and she signed it without even looking. "Now, Aunt Lisa, this is even more important: I need you to promise me that you won't talk to anyone about what happened that day. Don't talk to anyone about the murders. Please, never again tell anyone that you killed the girls—no police officers and no lawyers, even if they say they're here to help you. Have no more conversations with Judith, and certainly no judges. And absolutely don't talk to anyone from the newspapers. From now on, you talk only to me. If someone says you have to talk to them, tell them that your lawyer said not to. Get them to call me. You know my cell number."

Now, just how was she going to explain this next part to her?

"I have another very important thing to ask you. It may sound strange, but it's very important. If Uncle Hill comes in to see you, please don't tell him what we talked about. We need to have a trustworthy attorney-client relationship." She hated to say this about her own uncle, but it just had to be this way. "One other thing. You're a strong woman, and I need you to stop taking whatever medication the doctor is giving you. No more pills. Just say no, and explain that your lawyer told you not to take anything. I need your mind sharp. Do you understand?"

Lisa nodded. "Yes, I understand, and I will. Sally, does this mean you're my lawyer no matter what anyone else says?"

"Yes. I am your attorney."

Sally sighed. *At least until I can get you a better one,* she thought.

"Thank you for coming, dear," Lisa said again with her slightly drugged-up grin. "Now I know everything will be all right."

Sally looked at her pleadingly, then hugged her and walked away.

CHAPTER FOUR

ACCIDENT OR ATTEMPTED MURDER?

Sally stood on the curb by the edge of the sidewalk. The past couple of hours had been mind-boggling, and the day was far from over! She already felt as though it had been three days long.

Suddenly, she noticed a cab approaching in the centre lane. She stepped out onto the roadway, ready to hail the vehicle over, when a bit of wind brushed up against her. The next thing she knew, she was sitting on the curb, having gone down with a jolt.

Her bones seemed to quiver for a moment, her stomach turning and her head whirling. She felt like a fool and the first thing she did was look around her. Thank goodness no one had seen her fall. She wasn't the clumsy type. It must have been a symptom of all the strain she was under. She had to be more careful.

She was just trying to pick herself up when a man appeared at her elbow.

"Are you okay?" he asked. "That driver must be a maniac. If I didn't know better, lady, I'd say he was deliberately trying to run you over. You got an enemy like that?"

"No, I don't think so. Thank you for helping me up. What happened?"

"That man near ran you over, just came out of nowhere. I tried to get his license, but the plate was too dirty. I'm sorry. But it was a light green Ford Taurus. Don't know the year, but fairly new. He must have been in one hell of a hurry. You can call the cops if you want. I'll tell them what happened."

"I'm sure it was an accident. Everyone's in such a hurry these days."

"Come on, my cab is at your disposal." He took her arm and helped her into the back seat of his cab, which was marked nearby. "One can't be too careful. You're right, everyone is in such a hurry. It's a wonder more people aren't hurt."

She told him where she wanted to go, and within minutes they were on their way.

After a short drive, the cab slowed down and the driver turned around in his seat, surprise written on his face.

"Ma'am, are you sure this is where you want to be?"

She nodded. "Yes, this is the place."

"Well, ma'am, the entrance is packed with news media. I think it's the home of that judge and his wife who they're holding for murder. Are you visiting friends here?"

She wasn't going to explain that the judge was her uncle.

"Ma'am, there's a rear entrance and a freight elevator that goes up the back of the building. If you want, I can drive you around back."

Thank you, Lord.

"I appreciate that more than you know," she said, feeling tired. She really couldn't go through all those reporters. Hopefully there wouldn't be security at the back to stop her.

The cabby drove right by all the reporters and headed for the back alley, where he stopped.

"That door right there," he said, pointing. "Just hit the red button on that small panel and you can get the security guard. He'll let you in."

"Will you hold on a minute until I'm sure? I don't want to be stuck out here alone."

"Yes, ma'am."

Sally walked up to the door, shoved her driver's licence up to the little glass window, and waited.

"Come in, Ms. Cameron," the security guard said. "I was told you might return."

She rid herself of another two twenties and waved at the driver as he left.

A few moments later, Sally found herself inside a long hall, facing an elevator. She hated the contraption; it looked like a cage. She sighed, thinking that this would be a test of her courage.

She walked inside and pulled a thick rope to close the cage-like door behind her.

Soon she had arrived at the tenth floor. Once the door was open, she was out of the cage as quick as a flash. One thing she knew for sure was that she wasn't riding that contraption back down again.

She made her way along the corridor and came to a stop in front of her uncle's door. She almost dreaded going inside, for fear of what she might find there. Her uncle had been in bad shape earlier, although he'd had plenty of time to sober up by now.

If I were in his shoes, I would be embarrassed beyond words that my niece saw me in that condition, she thought.

She knocked the little brass knocker a couple of times. When the door opened, there stood her uncle, big as life. He clasped her in his arms and gave her cheek a kiss. He looked so normal now, the spitting image of her own father.

"It's so good so see you, my dear," he said. "You're as beautiful as ever. Sally dear, please come right into the sitting room. Have you seen your aunt? I am so worried about her."

"Yes, I have. She's actually doing remarkably well."

CHAPTER FOUR: ACCIDENT OR ATTEMPTED MURDER?

Anna appeared from out of the kitchen.

"I am so glad your back," Anna said. "Maybe now he'll stop pacing the floor. He's wearing out the carpet and driving me crazy."

She noticed that Anna spoke of him as if she were scolding a child. She also got the impression that Anna hadn't told him Sally had seen him in his earlier condition, passed out.

"Come on, you have to eat and get something in your stomach," Anna added.

"You know, Anna's cooking is the best," her uncle raved. "She's outdone herself for you, my dear. Come." He took Sally's arm. "We'll be able to talk after dinner. I have so much I want to explain to you."

She hadn't been hungry at first, but the amazing aroma of dinner soon changed her mind. She decided she must be starving.

"Now, my dear, please come into the sitting room where we can talk more comfortably," her uncle said after dinner.

The two walked into the sitting room and sat in large easy chairs before the gas fireplace, watching each other closely.

"I really don't know where to start," he began. "So much has happened since we last saw you. It seems like a lifetime ago. I don't know if you're aware how dreadful the press has been to us, but there's been some very bad publicity. Makes the family look bad. The first thing I did was call your father. What was I to do?" He shook his head, unbelieving. "He told me you were already on the way, that Lisa had called you. It was such a relief to talk to your father. We've always been close. But then again, twins usually are." He paused, looking conflicted. "I feel I must tell you exactly what happened to make your aunt kill those girls. I must make you see how much I love her, and that what I'm doing is for the best."

Those words—*what happened to make your aunt kill those girls*—sounded so shocking coming from him.

"I suppose you have a hundred questions, and I can't blame you for that. I can tell you, Sally, that I hardly know what's real anymore."

"I'm sure you're under a great deal of strain, Uncle Hill," Sally said. "Maybe, in order for me to understand, it would help for you to start at the beginning and tell me how Aunt Lisa became involved with these two prostitutes in the first place."

"You see, my dear, it started about two weeks ago. I always finish up early on Fridays, like clockwork. I play eighteen holes of golf with the other judges and then we meet at the country club at three o'clock. Well, as I approached my car, I noticed a sleek little red sports car parked right behind it. As I came closer, I saw two young women bent over the open hood. I decided they must be having car trouble, so I stopped and offered to help. That's when I realized they must be street girls, from the way they were dressed.

"'Just what are you two up to?' I asked. 'Stealing cars carries a serious charge, much worse than prostitution.'

"The one girl spoke, as nice as you please, asking me to help them with their car. 'It's not stolen. I have the registration and can prove it.'

"Well, it was true. The car belonged to her. To make a long story short, the girl surprised me by coming up with a plan to get the car running again. She asked me to sit in the driver's seat and press on the gas while they gave it a push. I couldn't get my own car out of the lot until theirs was moved, you understand, so I didn't have a choice. But their car did eventually start, and I was so relieved.

"When I tried to get out of the silly thing, though, my long legs wouldn't cooperate. Before I knew what was happening, she was almost on top of me. She thanked me, then hugged me and gave me a kiss right on the mouth. Her hands were all over me. Her neckline was low and she seemed somewhat exposed. I was

CHAPTER FOUR: ACCIDENT OR ATTEMPTED MURDER?

very embarrassed. I can't tell you how glad I was when I finally got free of the car and the girls." He chuckled. "If I had been twenty years younger, I might have enjoyed the incident.

"Several days later, I found out the same two girls were trying to blackmail me. Can you believe it? Some pictures had been taken without my knowledge. One girl actually showed them to Judith Alves, of all people, to make sure I paid up.

"'You won't want to see these pictures,' Judith told me. 'And no one will ever have to see them.'

"The pictures were taken so close up that you couldn't even tell they were taken in a car. Sally, I certainly didn't want to pay them one cent! I thought that might be the end of it, but no."

Sally stared at him in surprise. "Uncle Hill, didn't you notice someone with a camera nearby?"

"No, I didn't. It all happened so quickly. Besides, I was too busy to worry about a camera." He paused. "This is one of those times when hindsight does no good. Anyway, Lisa found out about the pictures, too, when one of the girls called her. The girls knew I wouldn't pay, but they still wanted money. So Lisa made arrangements to meet the girls at their apartment, saying she was willing to pay the blackmail. Instead she killed them! Lisa told both Judith and the police that it wasn't the girls' lifestyle that upset her, but the blackmail." He drew a deep, shuddering breath. "Now you know all that I know."

"Uncle Hill, I wish I knew what to say. My heart goes out to you. So often the public feels sorry for the victims, never knowing the pain the perpetrator's family goes through. I've sat and cried with families who have seen loved ones go to prison, and they have no understanding of how it happened." Sally sighed. "Having heard your side of the story, I suppose it makes sense. But I have to ask you one more time, and please, please be honest with me: do you honestly believe Aunt Lisa killed those prostitutes?"

"Yes, I do. Sally, that's exactly why you can't get involved in this mess. You're only going to hinder her. It's too personal. You refuse to accept the truth because you care for her so much, can't you see?"

Sally wore a puzzled expression on her face. "Uncle Hill, what if Aunt Lisa thought she was doing you a favour? Wasn't she trying to protect you?"

"She's a darn fool if she thought that." The anger was evident in his voice. "No, I don't believe she killed them trying to protect me. She may have thought there would be no end to the blackmail. She may have decided not to give them her money. You know, there was a side to your aunt you never knew. Lisa handled all the money and she could be very tight-fisted with it when she wanted to be."

"Do you know the time of death?" Sally asked.

"Around three-thirty in the afternoon."

"Were DNA samples taken from the crime scene?"

"I'm not sure. That would be up to the police," he said. "You seem to be ignoring the stress Lisa has put on me during this past few months. I'm telling you, if this isn't settled quickly, the Cameron name will be dragged through the muck. Your father won't like that one bit and I'll lose my job as a judge."

Sally nodded. "Uncle, I have another question. Why haven't you hired an actual defence attorney to represent her?"

"I'm so glad you brought that up. I have to be honest with you, my dear, and say that I've talked this over with Ben Purveys. He agreed we can settle this very easily. We have some friends who will do a good job. The only problem is determining which one would be best."

"I'm sorry, I don't follow you."

"My dear, understand that this is strictly to do with Lisa and myself and what I think is best for her. Judith said you would want to represent your aunt, but it has nothing to do with you. You may be a top lawyer in your field, but I think you're too close to this. Your father agrees that it would look better for your aunt if you didn't play a part in this. He suggested that you get on the next plane home and forget the whole thing. Until then, I was thinking you might be more comfortable staying in a hotel."

Sally almost laughed. *So you don't want me around, Uncle? Something just isn't right here.*

"Well, now that you mention it, I've already made other plans. But I didn't want to hurt your feelings." She stood up, but stopped before leaving the sitting room. "Before I go, Uncle Hill, just know that you don't need to get a lawyer for Aunt Lisa. I've taken care of that through a friend of mine who lives here."

Lord, forgive the lie, she thought. *Wow, I've never done this much lying my whole life.*

For some reason, she felt the need to be dishonest with him. She also felt the need to get out of there—fast, although she didn't know where she was going next.

She grabbed her bag, which contained the newspapers and the piece of paper she'd gotten her aunt to sign earlier. Then she thanked Anna, who was standing near the door with a woebegone look on her face.

"I'll be in touch," Sally said, smiling at them both as she left.

The apartment door closed behind her as she started walking down the hall, feeling terribly uncomfortable. She had too much heartache to make any big decisions right now, but she needed to find a quiet place where she could read, and maybe even cry for a bit.

Certainly there was no way she could have stayed there. She needed a private place where people couldn't snoop on her as the case progressed. She couldn't work out of the library, which would be too public, and a hotel room was definitely out of the question.

She'd have to leave all sorts of documents and legal papers in her room, and for a few bucks anyone could sneak inside. No, a hotel room wouldn't hold any secrets.

What she wouldn't give to have been able to stay out of this!

Somewhere in the book of James was a verse that came to mind: *"If any of you lacks wisdom, let him ask of God, who gives to all liberally and without reproach, and it will be given to him. But let him ask in faith, with no doubting, for he who doubts is like a wave of the sea driven and tossed by the wind."*[1] She had never been any good at remembering exactly where these things could be found.

Lord, something is very wrong here, she prayed. *But you brought me here, to do the right thing. I need your help. Thank you.*

She didn't know if she had gotten all the words right, but she knew exactly what she needed right now: wisdom.

---

[1] James 1:5–6

CHAPTER FIVE
MEETING PETER

Sally had never been so confused. Her head ached, and it seemed like today had been the longest day of her life. She was getting close to that point in time when she'd have to crash. She stopped for a moment to think. What was she going to do? Privacy was so important. Maybe she would have to settle for a hotel after all, at least for the next couple of days. Her very tired body and feet took her to the lobby of the building and then over to the waiting security guard.

"Sorry to bother you," she said. "I need to find a hotel. How is the one across the street?"

He looked her over, very obviously reaching the decision that it wasn't for her. "You might like to try the Hotel Saskatchewan instead. Any cab driver will take you there." He paused, staring at her. "You're the one who came in through the back door, right?"

"Yes, I did, to avoid the press."

She walked away from the man, dragging her bag. She felt like she was loaded down with newspapers. As she peeked outside, though, she couldn't believe her eyes: there was no sign of reporters. They must have given up for the day.

She left the building, once again thankful for small mercies, then stopped at the curb and took careful aim where she was going. She made sure this time that it was safe to cross the busy road.

Sally made her way to the hotel across the street, despite the bad recommendation. After walking through the large, wide glass doors, she found a line payphones. She decided to walk past them into a coffee shop. A few more minutes wouldn't make any difference.

The place was nearly empty, so she sat at the counter, dumping her luggage at her feet and the newspapers on the stool beside her. She had wanted a booth, but it was safer here, out in the open. Anyway, she would be on her way in a few minutes.

"Coffee, miss?" asked the waiter, a handsome young man.

"Yes, thanks. I don't suppose you have a nice, sweet piece of pie? I really need a drop of energy."

"Sure, miss. Angie makes her own pies. We have a coconut cream that would melt the stoniest heart."

"Perfect." She unburdened herself of her small purse, putting it on top of the newspapers. She took a deep breath and let it out very slowly, relaxing for the first time in what seemed like forever.

She leaned back, thankful for the stool's comfortable back. She was so tired. She ached everywhere. Without too much trouble, she thought she could sleep right here.

Once the coffee and pie arrived, she took a sip, and then a bite. Surprisingly enough, it was delicious. With every mouthful, she began to feel somewhat better. She hoped it would chase away the headache that was threatening to explode any minute.

After a few minutes, she couldn't ignore the feeling that someone was watching her. A man was seated further down the counter, a few stools away, and she had paid him no attention. Now she was sure he was being very careful not to get caught looking. If there was one thing she didn't need, it was some guy trying to pick her up.

After a few minutes more, he moved closer to her.

CHAPTER FIVE: MEETING PETER

Oh no, she thought. *He's not getting the message. Hopefully he's not some drunk. Haven't I had enough for one day?*

She sighed, trying to look unapproachable.

"Excuse me," he said, raising his hand to ward her off. "Now, don't hit me or scream for the cops. I'm a good guy, I promise. Are you by any chance related to Judge Cameron? Don't bite me, friend. I saw you go to the back of the building in a cab a few hours ago, and I've been sitting here ever since having a contest with myself to see whose side you're going to take. I figured if you stayed in for the night, you would be on his side. Am I right?" He offered a pleasant smile. "I was positive that would be the proof, the crucial point, of where you stood in this whole affair. Sorry, that's bad wording."

"Where I stood?" Sally's brow creased. "What exactly does that mean?"

"If you had left in a cab, I would have followed you. I was hoping we could make a deal. I'm a truthful kind of guy, so you might listen to me. I have my own opinion on the case."

"A deal. Well, I have to admit, your approach is… different," Sally said. "Exactly who are you and what do you do?"

"My name is Peter Matthews and I work for one of the papers here in the city." He put his hand up again, as Sally looked ready to bolt. "Wait, hear me out. I've never met your aunt, although several of my friends have. I'm part Cree Indian and proud of my ancestry. You would probably like me to tell you my name is Big North Star or something like that, but you'll have to settle for plain old Peter Matthews."

He took out his wallet and produced his driver's licence, health card, and library card.

"I hope this tells you I'm on the up and up," he added.

Sally looked at his cards, then handed them back. "You don't necessarily look Cree."

"Now don't tell me you have something against Canada's Aboriginal people?"

"Of course not. I know there are many people with Indian ancestry who live in Regina. My aunt had a real love for your people. She's made a lot of friends among you."

"Good. Does that mean you'll talk to me?"

"Of course I will. Just remember that you're a stranger to me."

She looked into his eyes, trying to see into his soul. She was usually good at judging a person after a few glances, but this fellow was very difficult to read. Yet something inside her said she could trust him.

"I write fiction when I'm not chasing a story," Peter said. "I've been quite successful, selling seven books and quite a few poems. I own my own home and help people when I can. So I can't be all bad!"

"All right, I accept that. I'm still questioning why you're interested in me. You also seem very well informed, and that implies you're working an angle. What if you're wrong about these so-called opinions?"

"Simple. Then I'm up and out of here, just like that." He paused. "And you can forget my offer of a good lawyer to help your aunt. I did hear, from a little birdie, that you saw your aunt earlier today. I have some friends in high places."

She's nothing like I expected, Peter thought to himself. *She's very attractive.*

He also noticed the huge rock on her ring finger. Private property. That was too bad. Then again, that was the story of his life.

"Look, I would like to be honest with you and come right to the point. You see, there are many people in this city who don't believe Mrs. Cameron killed anyone. But you'll have a problem getting her a good lawyer, so I have a deal for you."

CHAPTER FIVE: MEETING PETER

"What kind of deal?"

"I'll get you the best defence attorney in Regina, someone who already believes she didn't do it. While there are some good ole boy judges in charge of things, and they're ready to defend your uncle, there are people on the other side. We need you and you need us. That's the way I see it." He took a sip from his coffee cup. "We're convinced there are a few men in prominent circles who are involved with these girls. I know how that sounds, but in our experience men in high places are just as guilty of fooling around as normal, everyday men. The only difference is that the men in high places tend to get away with it."

"To be honest with you, I do need a good lawyer right now," Sally said. "I haven't had a chance to get all the information I need. I won't say much more, except that I'm going to make sure my aunt doesn't go to prison for something she didn't do."

She liked Peter, and liked that he cared to present himself so well. Most newsmen would have only cared about the story. That said, she wasn't sure if she trusted him.

"The word on the street is that these bigshots are bringing in an out-of-town judge to do the deed. No jury. Another group of people in the city won't let that happen. We feel your aunt is being railroaded." Peter looked around at the almost empty restaurant. "We have a lot more to talk about, but ears are everywhere. Let's sit in a booth where we can speak more privately. Please trust me."

Sally did want to hear what else he had to say, and it was true that he might be able to help.

"All right." She stood, gathered her belongings, and carried them to a booth of her own choosing. They sat down across from each other, each holding coffee mugs.

"I can see you're as sceptical as I am," he began. "I can help you if you're sincere. If not, I'm your enemy. But I have to be sure you want to hear the truth." He hoped she was following along.

"I'm here for one reason only: to see that whoever killed those girls pays. That's not your aunt. Now, I don't care who it turns out to be. The problem here is, you might."

The waitress came by and set a full carafe of coffee on the table.

"If you want anything else, just whistle." She smiled, then walked back to the counter.

Peter began filling the mugs once they were alone again. "There's nothing better to talk over than hot coffee." He took a drink. "Are you following me?"

"I have to tell you, I'm so tired I can barely think straight. How do I know that what I say to you won't end up on the front page of the paper in the morning?"

"You don't," he admitted. "What I can promise is that what we talk about won't end up in my paper without you knowing about it first. Now, if you're going to help your aunt, then honestly, you need help from the local people who know what's going on. Am I right?"

"Yes, you're right." She gazed into his eyes, and found that she rather liked what she saw. "What is this assistance going to cost? And please don't say nothing. If we're going to be partners in this arrangement, I want the truth."

"Look at it this way." Peter smiled at her. "If you give me the exclusive rights to the story, and permission to make it into a book when it's over, I'll get you a good lawyer and a terrific bunch of good cops who will help you find the real killer. And I won't print anything you don't want in the paper. Not only that, but I can lead you to a perfect safe house where no one will find you, a safe and secure place where you can work your heart out. I can also supply you with a vehicle. I'll help in any way I can." He grinned again. She was starting to get used to it. "Not a bad offer, if you honestly think about it."

He hoped she would take it; he wanted her where he could keep an eye on her. When she found out who the bad guy was, anything might happen. In the meantime, they needed her too.

"I have to admit, that's an offer I can't refuse," she said. "However, I'm sure you can understand my suspicion of you. I know what newspapers do to sell copies. I also know what newspaper reporters do to get headlines! Right now I have little choice, though. I'm desperate." She gave him a long, hard look. "You have a deal. If you double-cross me, I'll get even. I promise you that."

"I'll accept that for now." He chuckled. "And remember that trust is a two-way street."

She walked out of the coffee shop, following this stranger and wondering if she was losing her mind. Peter carried her luggage and all the newspapers.

At least the waitress saw us leave together, she thought. *A killer at large, and here I am, alone, about to trust a stranger!*

"My chariot, ma'am." Peter opened the passenger door of a very nice black car. He then put her things on the backseat and got behind the wheel, fastening his seatbelt. "My newspaper income didn't purchase this baby, my latest book did."

He started the car, taking off rather quickly.

Sally touched her purse and felt the little gun inside that went everywhere with her these days.

"The safe house isn't that far, although nothing is far when you're in Regina," he pointed out. "How long has it been since you were last here?"

"Almost ten months," she said, smiling. "I've been visiting my aunt and uncle regularly ever since I was twelve."

Sally stared straight ahead as they roared down the highway, seeming to leave the city.

"Don't panic," he said, as though sensing her concern. "We're coming up to a road that runs through some farmland. That's where I live. You're in safe hands."

They turned off the road, fields stretching out in all directions.

"You're one gutsy woman to trust me," Peter said. "Sorry, I'm just teasing you."

Suddenly, the car turned onto a paved driveway. Up ahead was a lovely older home with a sprawling yard. It had a friendly look.

"Come on, out you get." Peter opened the door for her. "This way, ma'am. Believe me, you'll love it here. It's nothing like the city, with all its new buildings."

She got out, clutching her bag. "Please, call me Sally. My friends all do."

"Thanks, I will." He picked up her things. "Try to unwind. You're going to need to relax."

He got to the front door and just walked in. No locks, no keys.

"I don't worry about prowlers out here," he said, noticing her look of surprise. "Almira, honey. Where are you all at?"

Sally frowned. Who was Almira? A dog or cat? Just then, an older woman appeared, hurrying down the hall toward them. She was chubby and small, clad in large teddy bear slippers. A flowered housecoat flowed about her as she bustled toward them. She shone with happiness to see Peter.

"This little ole lady is Almira," Peter said by way of introduction. He spoke in an affected southern drawl. "From the south of Georgia."

They both laughed at the shared joke. It was easy to see that she most definitely was not from the south. She had a distinctly Cree look.

"Almira, this here is another southern belle by the name of Sally."

"Now don't you pay him any attention, ma'am," Almira said, speaking softly and with a great deal of affection. "He likes his little jokes. We're both very proud of our heritage, although it's sure hard to keep our traditions these days."

CHAPTER FIVE: MEETING PETER

Peter nodded at her. "Sally's going to stay with us for a while, Almira. If you need some extra help, you can ask Fred. We're going to put together a makeshift office for the lady while she's here." He turned on the fake accent again. "Almira, my darling, I know you can keep a secret. We're not telling anyone that she's here—absolutely no one. In fact, you'll be interested in knowing that this lady is here to help Lisa Cameron."

The chubby little woman looked her over. It seemed to Sally that she could see right into her soul.

"Lisa Cameron is my aunt and a very special person to me," Sally said. "I know she didn't kill those two girls, and I plan on seeing that she isn't held responsible for it. We need to clear her name."

Peter handed Almira the newspaper. "Almira, follow us with these papers. I'm putting Sally in my mother's room."

"Yes, sir."

Almira didn't know what to think of this. Peter never brought girls home—and this girl seemed special. The niece of Mrs. Cameron! Now that was interesting.

"We have an unusual style of house," Peter explained as they walked through it. "My mother wanted it spread out, so that's what we have. It's a devil to heat in the winter. Mother thought fireplaces were the answer, and of course they weren't. If I ever get enough money, we'll try another form of heating. It's only comfortable during the summer." He paused as memory seemed to come over him. "My father died four years ago, and my mother three years ago. It was one of those cases where she couldn't live without him. They were old when they had me, and both were great parents."

Peter stopped at the open door to a bedroom, then led the way inside. The walls were painted a soft, buttery yellow.

"Everything you could want is here, so help yourself." He pointed to a closed door. "There's a washroom there."

He turned to leave.

"Sleep well," he added. "Almira will bring you a hot tea to help you get a good night's sleep. We'll talk in the morning. Good night."

Just like that, he was gone, Almira following behind him. Sally stood a few minutes looking at the closed door and wondering how she had ended up here.

Wait a minute, a voice inside her said. *You of little faith, didn't you ask God for a miracle? It would serve you right if he suddenly took it away, never mind that he said he would never leave or forsake you. So thank him, you idiot.*

Sally got down on her knees before the bed and did just that.

Afterward, she decided she was ready for bed. No matter how strange things were, she needed her sleep. She took the small gun from her bag and slipped it under the pillow. There was no fool like a thirty-year-old fool!

Exhaustion soon gave way to sleep.

CHAPTER SIX
PIECING IT TOGETHER

Sally's eyes opened to an unfamiliar sight, and panic hit her for a moment—until she remembered where she was. As she sat up on the edge of the bed, she heard the familiar sound of rain splattering against the room's large window.

She had so much to do today that she barely knew where to start. She was still exhausted from yesterday. She reached over to the night table and picked up her wristwatch. She looked at it three times before she could believe what her eyes were telling her: it was ten o'clock in the morning. She had never slept that late on a weekday.

Sally made her way into the washroom and had a quick shower. In no time, she was dressed in jeans a bright orange shirt and her hair was dry. A ponytail would have to do this morning until she figured out what was going to do with the day. She had several places to go—and she was dreading it.

"Are you up yet?" Almira asked through the closed door.

"Yes, I am." Sally rose to her feet and opened the door. Almira's smiling face greeted her. "Good morning, Almira. I see it's raining."

"Probably just a shower. We never complain about rain. The farmers always need rain on the prairie. There's never much rain in Regina, the land of the big sun."

"I know, it's wonderful. I love your province very much."

"I thought I'd better come and show you the way to the kitchen. Boss says I should set breakfast in the dining room. He's gone to the newspaper to get everything he can about your case. That's what he said. I was to be sure and tell you. Oh yes, he'll hurry back soon. And you should stay put until he comes back. His word." She threw her arm in the direction of the dining room. "This way."

Sally followed Almira towards the back of the house. The first thing she noticed was that the woman took her to the kitchen, not the dining room.

"Please sit down and I'll get you breakfast," Almira said.

Sally sat down as the woman was staring at her.

"Is there something wrong?" Sally asked.

"You're the first lady the boss ever brought here, since his mother died. You must be special. You love the boss?"

Sally thought the woman's question was a little spooky and she didn't know how to answer it. She just smiled. It was easier than an explanation.

Almira turned and hurried to the long counter. In minutes she was back, putting coffee down on the lovely green and yellow printed placemats that sat on the old polished walnut table. It was a beautiful piece of furniture.

"Is the kitchen okay?" Almira asked. "Boss said we should use the dining room. I could take you there, but it's large and not so nice when it's raining. The boss always eats in the kitchen for breakfast. Puts him in a better mood. Happy, you know."

"I see. This is just fine. Please, you don't have to go out of your way for me. I appreciate having someplace to stay where it's quiet and I can work. This really is a lovely kitchen."

Almira served a superb breakfast. After they'd eaten, Peter walked up to the table and sat down. Almira immediately jumped up and brought him a hot coffee.

"You want anything? Maybe a nice soft biscuit?" Almira asked. "We thought it was nicer here. It's too dark in the dining room."

"You just didn't want to disturb the dining room," Peter said, smiling. "I would like a biscuit, though. Thanks." He turned to Sally. "Good morning. I hope you slept well."

Sally nodded. "Yes, I did. Almira said that you left early. She's an amazing cook."

They both made small talk. In a few minutes, when breakfast was over, they made their way to the front of the house. Peter opened a French door that led into a large sunroom. The huge glass windows were curtained with long slated blinds, open to great fields full of golden wheat, glimmering as far as the eye could see. The rain had stopped and the sun was proclaiming its glory over the distant city.

"I've laid out two foldup tables for you. Personally, I find this arrangement easy to work in. I've also set up a computer and printer." Peter lifted up an empty briefcase from the table and handed it to her. "I gave you an old one. Thought it would make you look more experienced."

She knew what he meant. Pens and pencils were in evidence, as well as lots of loose paper and several file folders in different colours.

"The printer is ready, with paper already in it," he continued, looking out the window at the bright sunshine. "If there's anything else you want, just ask. Nobody will bother you out here. It's yours as long as you need it. No one, absolutely no one, will touch anything, and no one knows you're here. I want to keep it that way so you have complete privacy."

"Peter, this is wonderful. I don't know how I'll ever thank you."

He smiled and led her away to see the rest of the house. "I have another special place you might as well find your way to. Follow me."

She followed him back along a hallway. He opened the door at the end, which opened into a huge library. The walls were covered in bookshelves. A sizable walnut desk sat in the corner alongside a large television.

"I love books, as you can see, and TV too," he said.

Sally saw that he had arranged another corner almost the same way, with a computer and mounds of books and paper. She had never experienced such a peaceful feeling. It was pure luxury, warm, desirable, and useful.

"Peter, this is a perfect sanctuary. I love it."

"Thank you, Ms. Cameron. Coming from you, that is indeed high praise." He bowed as he spoke, then pointed to a shelf of leather-bound oldies. "Over there is my passion."

That doesn't surprise me, she thought, coming to the conclusion that there was certainly some money tied up in this collection of old books.

What gorgeous eyes she has, he thought, trying not to dwell on the ring on her finger. *I like this woman very much.*

"Are you sure you're up to this?" Peter asked. "You're not going to change sides on me halfway through?"

"No. I'm here to do a job and that means I'll do anything to save my aunt. I'm ready and I have a lot to do today. I'll need some transportation later, though."

"I've got a car you can use." He pulled out a chair next to his desk. "Sit thee down, my lady. Do you want to hear about my early morning visit to the city?"

She sat down, although the chair was a little too close to him for her liking.

"Okay, you should find this interesting. Just keep an open mind. Number one, your uncle has an apartment in the city—in addition to the condo where he lives with your aunt. Were you aware of this?"

CHAPTER SIX: PIECING IT TOGETHER

Sally sat back. "No, I didn't know. Two places? That's odd. Are you sure?"

"The apartment is in a large older home. The owner rents out rooms without requiring a paper trail. The rent is paid each month by cash. So whoever pays the rent obviously doesn't want their name on anything. And guess who supposedly lived there? Corey Pearl and Joanna Star, the two murdered girls."

"What! Are you serious?" Sally lifted her head in the air, completely shocked. Are you saying they lived in an apartment my uncle was paying for?"

"Yes. Hold on, I'll come back to them in a bit." Peter looked down at some notes he held in a small book. "To make things even more interesting, your uncle has a secret account at a local bank. Clare Agnew, his secretary, has yet another account in a different bank. Here's how the rent gets paid. Mrs. Agnew goes to the judge's bank, not her own, and gets the cash. Then she goes to the homeowner and pays the girls' rent. She takes out this exact amount from your uncle's bank account each month, one or two days before the rent is due. Never late, always on time—again, to avoid any hassle. Like I said, there's no paper trail or direct connection to the judge. Just the same withdrawal every month.

"Now, here's a bit of peculiar information. Another hooker, a friend of Joanna's, told me that apparently Mrs. Agnew objected to anyone else using the apartment. In other words, she insisted that she was paying for Corey to rent the apartment, not Joanna. And the more I learn about these two, the more interesting it becomes."

Sally was in complete awe, hanging onto every word he said.

"Mrs. Agnew would sometimes show up unannounced, as if to check on the girl. Apparently, these visits always ended in loud shouting matches, with Joanna immediately leaving and not coming back for a few days. It seems most of the arguments had to do with Joanna being there. I was curious where Joanna went during these incidents, and I figured out that she stayed at some guy's apartment in the same building. Then, when Corey gave her the all-clear, she would move back in, Joanna welcoming her with open arms. It does look as though those girls had more than friendship between them. Some kind of business relationship?

"As for Corey, she was somewhere around thirty-one or thirty-two years old. I checked around several schools and nobody seems to have heard of her, and her fingerprints don't reveal anything we don't already know. She was arrested for prostitution a few times, but the charges were always dropped in your uncle's court…"

Peter trailed off, giving Sally a strange look.

"What's the matter?" Sally asked.

"Don't get mad, but actually she looked a lot like you in many ways. Her complexion was a little darker, but otherwise the resemblance is uncanny. She drew attention wherever she went, at least from a distance, but up close, you could see the effects of hard living—drugs and drinking. She definitely worked as a prostitute, as far as the police are concerned, although she didn't have a pimp that we know of. I figure she must have had cover in high places."

He clicked his tongue, then changed the subject.

"Okay, let's look at the gun that killed the two girls. Did you know that it belonged to your uncle? Apparently he owns two guns, both of which are supposed to be for protection against burglars. One was kept in the sitting room, and the other in the night table drawer next to the bed. He has permits for both. Anyway, he claims that he had no idea the gun was missing, but when the police found it, it was covered with your aunt's fingerprints. Some of your uncle's as well. It was his gun, though, so that's to be expected. Although there were a few unidentified prints too, only smudges. That might come in useful later."

CHAPTER SIX: PIECING IT TOGETHER

"You know, Peter, this is unbelievable," Sally said, staring at him with wondering eyes. "Are you just trying to figure out how much shock I can take in one day? Needless to say, I didn't know any of this. Remember, I just arrived in town. I didn't even know he owned guns."

Peter shrugged. "Somehow I didn't think you knew. As I said, the gun is registered and all very legal. The big question, as I see it, is this: why were your aunt's prints on the gun, and who else had access to it? That brings us back to your aunt."

"I can't, for the life of me, see my aunt even touching a gun." Sally shook her head in confusion. "I would be willing to bet she never fired a gun in her life. No, there's something very odd with the possibility that she fired that gun. Peter, do you know if they checked for residue on her hands or clothing?"

"I understand it was too late by the time they arrested her," Peter said. "That's good news for our side. The bullets were aimed right at the girls' foreheads, and there weren't any stray bullets found. I would say the killer is a good shot. The whole killing was very neat—too clean for an old woman."

Sally's face brightened. "If she had never shot a gun before, that would be almost impossible, never mind the state of mind she must have been in. Peter, this is the best news I've heard today. I'll have to ask my aunt if she ever took shooting lessons. If she says yes, I'll find out where and what kind of a shot she was." She paused, wondering whether to reveal the truth about her own gun. "I have a gun, too, Peter, and I've had several lessons on how to fire it. I'm not a bad shot, but I probably couldn't hit right on a target unless I was quite close. Although I suppose these shootings were close-range."

"True." Peter sat up straighter. "Now we come to the matter of your aunt's signed confession. She refused to admit *how* the murders happened. Her statement simply says that she shot them, period. Her explanation was that she was too upset to notice or remember what happened. We think that a cop probably wrote the confession and then she signed it. It was all typed, very neatly of course, as is the usual practice."

Sally staring at him, her mind running in circles.

He cleared his throat. "Okay, next up: the blackmail pictures. I'll be honest with you: no one so far can find out what sort of pictures these are, or if the police actually have them in evidence. One minute they exist, and the next they seem not to."

"I'll visit my aunt again this afternoon," Sally decided. "I'm hopeful that she's in her right mind, as a lot depends on whether or not she took her prescriptions today. If all goes well, I should have more information tonight."

Peter was amazed at how well she was taking all the news. "There's also a man who has an apartment in the same building," he added. "The cops are after him all the time for selling drugs, but they can't seem to catch him in the act. The narcotics division watched the girls' place for over a month and decided they weren't worth the effort. So I'm told."

"That may be something for us to examine very carefully," Sally suggested.

He nodded. "Several times when Corey was arrested, she was as high as a kite on something very strong. She wouldn't tell the cops where she managed to get the stuff. She just admitted to getting it off the street. Also, Corey or Joanna always called a lawyer by the name of Ben Purveys. Whenever they did, they were let go fairly quickly."

Ben Purveys! Sally recognized his name from her conversations with her aunt.

"I have another idea," Peter continued. "I've heard that a mystery woman visited the apartment a few times, just flitting in and out. Probably to bring the girls drugs. Some people are saying that the woman was your aunt, who had a reputation for helping people in bad areas of town, which also means she could have gotten whatever drugs she needed. But I have to admit, if your aunt felt sorry for the girls because of their suffering, I'd be puzzled as to why she would bring them drugs."

Sally stared at him, slowly counting to ten before saying anything.

"I would normally say that's not possible, under any circumstances," she finally said. "But after my interview with her, anything is possible. But we're now presuming that she knew about this apartment for some time. We're also assuming that she knew about my uncle's affairs. What a mix of characters in this case!"

CHAPTER SEVEN
LISA'S STORY

After her meeting with Peter, Sally decided to visit her aunt again at the courthouse, hoping that she would be back to her old self.

"I'll see you here for dinner around seven," Peter said as he walked her to the garage. "If you get tied up, call and I'll understand. I know how important this is to you."

When they reached the large garage, Sally realized that it could have accommodated about six vehicles. One whole portion was dedicated to a workshop, a tractor, and large tools and machines. Across from this were parked three cars.

In no time, Sally had gotten into one of those cars and driven away.

Once she arrived at the courthouse, she made her way inside and walked to the end of the hall, dreading this visit. At least she expected to learn a great deal more about her aunt's condition and get some honest answers.

A policeman was sitting outside the door as a guard, just like yesterday. He looked to be about thirty. His copper hair, highlighted by the light coming in through a window, looked almost like a halo. He was bent over, reading a book that was open to the middle.

CHAPTER SEVEN: LISA'S STORY

Once he had let her in, Sally entered the comfortable cell and saw Lisa sitting in the yellow chair. She approached, then gave her aunt a hug and a kiss on the cheek.

"You're looking well," Sally said.

"I think I feel somewhat better, dear."

Sally took a deep breath. She was going to try another approach with her today. "I've had a busy morning and have to talk with you about something," Sally began. "I've decided that if you insist on saying that you killed those girls, you're going to have to prove to me that you did. I want you to go over every single detail of what happened. As a matter of fact, the police are looking for other suspects."

She hoped that would give her aunt a little something to think about. She also hoped to distract her, and the untouched food tray on the table would work.

"First you have to eat," Sally added, wanting to divert her aunt's attention. She kept her voice abrupt and a bit unfriendly. "Eat, Aunt Lisa!"

She was being deliberately mean, to get tough with her. Lisa's head suddenly rose as she made eye contact with Sally. Frowning, Lisa picked up her sandwich and took a bite, then chewed and swallowed.

"You mean it wasn't enough to sign that paper?" Lisa asked. "What does all that other stuff matter? Judith told me that was all I had to do—"

"Now let me get this straight. You told me yesterday that you wouldn't talk to anyone. You promised me you were through talking to her. Why are we back to you taking her word for something this important? Explain this to me. I don't even think you like her."

"Oh, Sally, that was a couple of days ago. I've lost track of time in here." Lisa looked slightly disgusted. "Hill said I could trust Judith and to cooperate with whatever she said."

57

"So you mean you last spoke with Judith before our talk yesterday. Right?"

"That's right."

Sally nodded. "Okay. Please eat. No matter what happens, you're going to need your strength."

"I am eating." As Sally watched, Lisa consumed mouthful after mouthful. "You know, I'll say this: wherever they get their food from, it's very good. Quite delicious, actually. Filled with onion and celery and a touch of carrot."

Sally wanted to smile. Maybe she just needed to make her aunt a little peeved in order to get her to fight for what was right. Obviously she was unaware of what her so-called friends were up to.

Before too long, the tray was empty.

"Okay, it's time you and I secured some facts," Sally said. "I need you to tell me the truth. No more talk about what Judith or your husband said. I've heard a lot of versions about what happened, or what people think happened. Only you actually know what took place that afternoon, so that's what I'm after now." Before her aunt could speak, she put up her hand. "Now hear me out. I've been talking to some people who are going to help us, people who have nothing to do with your husband or his people. I need you to understand that when a case goes to court for a first hearing, several things take place. First, all kinds of terrible stories from the past are going to come to the surface. These can be difficult to deal with. People are going to testify against you in court. If your story and theirs is different, we're in trouble. I need to know anything that may come up in a courtroom. And don't tell me that you killed those girls. That won't wash with me. I know someone else is responsible, and it would be helpful if we could find out who they are. That would make my job a lot easier." For a while, her aunt said nothing. "If you insist that you killed them, then I want you to tell me exactly how you came to the point of planning their

CHAPTER SEVEN: LISA'S STORY

deaths and then exactly how you did it. Tell me why and how. Give me something to work with."

Lisa sighed, lowering her head. "If you want to know the truth, I have to take you back to the year after I graduated university. Your uncle and I had been married six months. Some people might call it an 'arranged marriage.' We were a couple of aristocrats who were ready to take our place in society. And this city accepted us with all the social graces of the wealthy. But it didn't take me long to learn that Hill was in love with a woman named Clare. Once, while he was supposedly travelling to Vancouver for a business deal, I found out that he was staying over at her place, that he wasn't in Vancouver at all. Well, I wasn't supposed to know and of course I never told a soul, out of embarrassment. After a while, I stopped caring…"

Lisa trailed off, falling silent. It seemed obvious to Sally that she was about to share something that was very difficult and painful.

"You should know that one of the dead girls was named Corey, and she was Hill's and Clare's daughter, the spitting image of her mother when she was young. As she grew up, she looked a great deal like you, my dear. It's no wonder Hill couldn't resist her. But I'll tell you more about her later." She took a breath, and then continued. "Hill climbed the social ladder quickly, working very hard to achieve success. I was always at his side, involved in all the charities and socials aspects of the city. Soon Hill started his own law firm and it grew very successful. We became well off on our own, and my father was proud of Hill. I think he really took him on as the son he never had."

Sally raised a finger. "Aunt Lisa, I'm sorry to interrupt, but I have a question. This Clare you keep talking about… is she the same woman who now works as Uncle Hill's secretary?"

"Of course. Who else? Clare had a degree and was more than equipped to be a legal secretary. She's worked for him all these years. So if you want to hear about Corey, you can see why I had to start at the beginning. I had to let you see how it was between the two of us. I'm sure Clare and I aren't the only women to have shared a man the way we did. It hasn't been easy, especially when Corey found out that Hill was her father. She tried to blackmail him several times. I do admit to feeling sorry for her and giving her money. Last month, though, she asked me for the money to buy an expensive little sports car—and I just snapped."

Lisa paused, her eyes losing focus as she looked off into nowhere.

"Sally, for the first time in my life I'd had enough, and I made up my mind to put an end to it. I even told Clare that she could have Hill, that I was filing for divorce that very day. Sally, I'm sorry. I really meant it. I was through. I told her I was going to get my own lawyer. It was over. But then Corey called me the next day and told me that she had those pictures and was going to give them to the newspapers unless Hill or I gave her more money than ever, and I refused."

"Do you know what happened to the pictures, Aunt Lisa?"

"No, but I presumed Hill had them."

"Aunt Lisa, how did your prints get on the gun?" Sally hated to ask that, but she needed to hear the truth. Maybe if Lisa really had killed the girls, they could offer a plea bargain.

Lisa sighed again. "After hearing about the pictures, I sat most of the next day trying to figure out what to do. Hill never came home that night. Well, I couldn't just ignore the whole thing, and I needed to get a lawyer who wasn't one of Hill's friends. I had no idea where to even start looking. That's when Hill called me and said that we needed to talk, that he would give me a divorce. Would I meet him at Corey's? Yes. I just wanted out.

"So I took a bus to the street were Corey lived. I walked past several houses before coming to the right one, a large home that had been split into apartments. Well, I had been there a few times before. As I came to the apartment door and tapped the brass knocker, the pressure of the small tap seemed to push the door open. I was surprised to discover that the door hadn't been closed tightly. I remember standing there, thinking this was odd.

"I pushed the door further open and walked in. I called for Corey, but no one responded. I just stood there, right inside the door. Understand that I was somewhat afraid of the girl, especially after her latest demands for money. Well, I eventually walked toward the kitchen and detected a terrible smell. I'm not sure what exactly went through my mind as I entered the kitchen, but that's when I saw both girls on the floor. I knew they were dead. There was some blood, not an enormous amount, but dark brown and some of it was stuck to the floor.

"At that point, I saw the gun. It lay on the floor next to Corey, and it looked like it had just fallen there. For a minute I thought they had killed themselves. Maybe Corey had shot Joanna, then herself. Maybe she'd done it because they had no money for drugs. But just as quickly I recognized the gun by its handle. Hill owned a set of matching guns that had been given to him several years ago with inlaid leather on the handles. It occurred to me that this had to be one of Hill's guns, because there wasn't another set like it. Stupid me, I really didn't think. I went over and picked up the gun, wanting to look at the handle more closely. Just as I was about to examine the gun, I blacked out.

"The next thing I remember, it was about twenty minutes later and I was on the floor with the gun in my hand. My eyes were blurry and I knew that if I didn't get to a washroom, I would throw up. I remember having trouble getting up off the floor. I was actually standing before I realized that I had the gun in my hand. I dropped it, of course, and headed for the washroom. I threw up, mostly just heaving. I washed my face and walked back into the kitchen, taking one last look to make sure I hadn't imagined the whole thing.

"As I stood there, I thought the worst thing you can imagine. I was glad. I really was glad. Then my senses returned and I realized that Hill must have killed the girls. Almost that very instant, Hill himself walked into the kitchen and demanded to know what I had done. I was so shocked to see him that I didn't say anything. 'Lisa, you've killed Corey and Joanna. Come on, we have to get out of here.' I wanted to say no, but I didn't. He took my arm, then stopped and said, 'We can't leave here together. You go first, and I'll follow. Hurry before the police come. Go straight home and we'll figure out what to do.'

"For a minute, I had no idea how to react, so I left as fast as my legs could carry me, praying that no one would see me. For the next few hours I lay in bed with hardly any memory of even going to that house. Hill assured me that I had killed the girls but that everything was going to be all right.

"Someone found the bodies a few hours after that, and then the police arrived and arrested me. I told the police that I had killed them, and that was that." Lisa buried her head in her hands. "You see, I couldn't live with Hill anymore. He said that I would go to jail for killing them, and there was so much evidence against me. He just explained that I must have been out of my mind and didn't remember killing them. Well, I just decided I would be better off in an institution, so I did what he and Judith suggested.

"I expect you can't understand how I feel. The anger is gone and I have nothing to live for now. Sally, the next time you see your uncle, tell him to get a good lawyer. I suppose he's going to need one. And will you also look into getting a divorce for me when you have a few minutes? I don't ever want to see Hill again. I should have done it years ago. Loving someone is actually a very painful thing. It makes you forgive too much." She shuddered, completely exhausted. "I think we've talked enough for today. I'm very tired."

Sally reached over and gave her a great hug.

"Thank you, Aunt Lisa, for telling me everything," Sally said. "Now I have to sort it all out and see where to go from here. One thing I do know is that we're going to have one unbelievable day in court. Just know that I still care about you, and I'm going to help you. I'm on your side. No matter what happens, please remember that in the next few weeks."

Sally stood up and gave her aunt an affectionate kiss on the cheek.

"You're a very considerate woman and altogether too good for Uncle Hill," Sally said.

Now what was she going to do? At least she had been right: her aunt hadn't killed anyone. But she'd gotten herself into something even more complicated.

I'll need time, Sally thought. *Lots of time—and Judith won't give it to me.*

CHAPTER EIGHT
THE MURDER SCENE

Sally was walking back to her car in the parking lot when she looked at her watch. It was a quarter to six. Although evening was about to set in, it still looked like midday.

Her feet ached in her high heels as she approached the car. Once inside, she rolled down the windows. The temperature outside was stifling and she found it was making it difficult to breathe.

She drove into the main stream of traffic, thinking about whether or not to call her father about the latest developments. She didn't want to talk to him; she wanted to know exactly where the case was going first. After all, she would need outside help and hadn't had the time yet to contact the man Peter had recommended.

Needing to make a call, she looked around for a place to pull over. After a few minutes, she pulled off the road into a shopping mall parking lot. She stopped the car and dialled a number on her phone.

"Hello," Almira answered. "Matthews residence. Who is this?"

"Almira, this is Sally. Will you give Peter a message that I'll be tied up for another two hours? Please eat without me."

"It's no problem. Anyway, the boss isn't here yet. See you when you get here."

The line went dead.

Some message-taker, Sally thought, smiling. Peter must have been tied up as well. At least it wouldn't be her fault alone that supper had to be warmed up.

Before she had left this morning, Peter had given her a map of the city. Now she looked over it, trying to find where she had to go next. Once she found the address, she started the car again and kept driving.

When she got close, she slowed down, taking her time as she watched the street names as she passed every road. She was looking for Cyanoses Drive, and not having any luck so far. Suddenly, while looking across to the far side of the road, she found it. The map hadn't said it only went one way! Here she was, trying to make time count, and she'd ended up on the wrong side of the street.

Sally had to make a U-turn and backtrack. She turned onto Cyanoses, then turned twice more, once to the right and then to the right again.

Finally, she pulled up to the curb along Wilfred Street, parked between two other cars. She cast her gaze up and down the quiet street. There was no one around, not even a dog-walker.

Should I be doing this? she asked herself. *Yes, I should definitely be doing this.*

Once she was sure that no one had followed her, Sally left the car and locked it. One step at a time, she made her way toward the house where the girls had been killed. As she walked, she took out her recorder and spoke into it, describing what she saw for later research.

All the houses in this part of the city had back lanes. She walked around back and looked around. The house next door had a wide veranda around the side. Maybe the neighbours would talk.

She walked onto the veranda of the house and rang the doorbell. It was a couple of minutes before an older woman answered the door.

"Yes, you want something?" the woman asked. She looked to be about sixty, five-foot-four, and Aboriginal. She wore a cotton housedress and slippers.

"I'm sorry to bother you. I'm investigating the murder next door. Would you be able to help me?"

"No, I can't and won't. I'm sick of the questions. Haven't you newspaper people seen and heard enough? Go away and leave us alone. Do you think I have nothing better to do than watch my neighbours?"

"I'm not from the police, and I'm not a reporter. I'm the lawyer for the woman who's been accused of the murder. Do you know Lisa Cameron? She's known for helping the poor and caring for the sick."

Go on, rub it in, thought Sally.

"I'm sure you're busy and I am sorry to bother you," Sally continued. "You see, it's very important. It would be deeply wrong if this good person goes to prison for something she didn't do while the real killer goes free."

The woman sighed. "Yeah, that's the wife of that judge. We all know her. She seems very nice, so it's too bad about her husband." She shook her head. "We have lots of street girls in this neighbourhood. Good girls, and it's sad when a couple of them get killed. Very bad. It wasn't always like this, you know. Times change, money talks, and there are drugs everywhere. It's not like the old days with the two-dollar bills."

Sally remembered hearing stories from the depression years about a two-dollar bill being famous for being a prostitute's fee.

Well, at least this woman was talking.

"Did you happen to see Mrs. Cameron go into the house next door last Wednesday?"

"No, can't say that I did. I wouldn't tell you anyway. That no good lazy Tony Clark was in and out a few times, though. He's a real bum, and he makes money off the girls. He's a real lowlife, and I wouldn't want him living in my house. Maybe he killed the girls!"

Sally raised an eyebrow. "Really? I haven't heard of him. What makes you think that?"

Maybe this was the stranger she was looking for. All she needed was one shred of doubt.

"Raven is crazy to let him live there," the woman said. "She says he pays the rent and that's all she cares about. As far as I'm concerned, the money isn't worth having that scum of the earth around. That fellow is bad news."

"Who's Raven?" Sally asked.

"Oh, that's the woman who owns the house next door."

Sally smiled, trying to keep the excitement out of her voice. "So you're saying this Tony guy lives in one of the apartments in her house?"

"Sure, right next door to Corey and Joanna. He's a real slime ball, into a lot of dirty stuff, and everyone around here knows it. The trouble is, some people are afraid of him. Not me."

"Thank you. I appreciate you telling me this," Sally said. "Now, I've heard there are a couple of older ladies who have been seen coming and going from Corey's apartment. Would you know anything about that?"

The woman shrugged. "I'm not a gossip, but Raven and I do talk over coffee sometimes. This happens here and that happens there, you get the idea. Anyway, yeah, there are two women who stop by—one in particular who might interest you. She brought the rent to Raven each month, paying for the girls' apartment. I think her name's Agnew, something like that. She's real heavy-handed and mean. Hard as nails, and rich. Corey's family has money, so maybe the two are related. Only the family has disowned her, or something like that."

"What do you mean, heavy-handed and mean?" Sally asked.

"She's hit Corey lots of times. Black eyes, bruises… you know. Raven even saw her do it. But those girls were asking for it, if you know what I mean. I know no one deserves to be killed, but they were trouble. I don't like Lisa Cameron being charged with the murder, though. She's not a bad lady."

Sally nodded. "You're right, no one deserves to be killed. What makes you think those girls were so bad, though?"

"Corey thought she was the queen bee. Lots of old guys would come and go, and she gave her favours for a lot of money. That friend of hers was no better, but Corey looked out for her, thinking she was better than everyone else. Corey was educated, not like the other street girls. She went to university. A lot of good it did her!"

The woman chuckled as though it were a joke.

Sally wondered how this woman knew so much about what went on in that house. Well, Sally thought she knew now where the newspapers received their material. But it wasn't necessarily the truth.

"What about the second woman?" Sally asked. "Can you describe her for me?"

"Sure. She's fair, medium height, dresses really well, looks like she came out of a magazine. She drives right up to the house and parks on the street, like she owns the place. She always wears a hat, as if that makes some difference. Raven can tell you more. I live too far away to describe the second woman better than that."

"Do you know her name?" Sally was fairly sure she knew who the second woman was.

"No. She's only come a few times."

"You mentioned the old guy who came to see Corey. Was there one who came around more often than the others?" Once again, Sally was pretty sure she knew the answer. She wanted to confirm it.

"Sure," the woman said. "He's been coming here forever and I can even tell you who he is: Judge Cameron. All the newspapers have it right. He's no good either. Funny how guys like him think they're so good all the time, but they're no better than we are."

"Are you sure it's Judge Cameron? I mean, how do you know for sure? Have you ever met him?"

"You don't believe me? Fine." The woman started to close the door.

"No, no, I didn't mean that. Please, I appreciate what you're telling me. If you say it was the judge, that's fine with me. I'm just surprised to hear that a judge would be coming around to see a hooker. You would think he might wear a disguise or something."

The woman opened the door again. "Like I said, he's been coming here for years. Everyone in the neighbourhood thinks it's a joke. These guys think they're above the law and don't need disguises." She hesitated. "Actually, though, he and his friends are a big help now and then. So we don't care what they do."

"Have you talked to the reporters about this?"

"Sure, everybody around here knows," she said. "And the girls are dead now, so it doesn't matter anymore. Some of the other girls won't get off so easy now. Corey used to make deals for them."

Sally nodded. "The day the girls were killed, did you by any chance see either of these women or the judge come or go from the house?"

"No. Like I told the police, I didn't see anything unusual that day."

"You must have seen Mrs. Cameron, though. She told me she was there in the afternoon. I'm just trying to find out the time she was there." She raised her hand like a Boy Scout. "I only want to help her, I promise."

"Look, I can't say much." She looked around, suspiciously. "Okay, I'll tell you, but no one else. Yes, I did see your lady. I saw the judge and another woman, too, but I can't tell you that in court. I won't say anything. I'm just telling you to help Mrs. Cameron. She left before the judge and the other lady did, as far as I know." The woman took a step back, her hand on the doorknob. "Mrs. Cameron didn't kill those girls, no matter what the papers say. You had better check on her husband. He more than likely did it."

The next thing Sally knew, she was staring at a closed door. That was that.

She turned the recorder off to save batteries, decided to listen back to the tape later to see if it was worthwhile. Who knew if she could trust what this woman had said? The problem was that her information was hearsay, and she wouldn't testify in court anyway. When it came right down to it, they wouldn't have a chance if nobody was willing to testify.

Sally turned and walked away, almost dreading to approach the house next door. She wondered if it would be a waste of time.

She walked along the sidewalk to the large house, not sure what to expect. She pressed the start button on her recorder as she walked up the front door. It wasted some of the tape, but that couldn't be helped.

She rang the doorbell and waited. Nothing happened.

Sighing once again, but not giving up, she rang the doorbell longer, with a heavier finger. Pretty soon she heard footsteps inside the house.

CHAPTER EIGHT: THE MURDER SCENE

The door opened and a tall, slender older woman stared out at her. Sally thought she was also of Aboriginal descent. She was dressed in a bright-coloured housedress with flowers on it. She'd draped a white sweater over her shoulders. Her bare feet were nestled inside slippers.

"What do you want?" the woman asked with a look of distrust. "We're sick of you people."

"I'm sorry to bother you, please don't close the door. It's very important that I talk to you. I'm the lawyer representing Lisa Cameron, the woman accused of killing two girls who lived here. I'm looking for the owner."

"Yeah, you got her. Raven Long Arrow Smith. I go by Raven Smith."

"How do you do, Mrs. Smith? I expect you must have known those girls, since they lived in your house. I'm sure you're as upset as can be. But you see, I know Mrs. Cameron didn't kill them." Sally noticed that Raven was given her the once-over, so she tried again. "I was just next door, and your friend said I should come and talk to you."

It was a small lie that couldn't be helped.

To Sally's surprise, the woman laughed heartily. "That must have been one waste of time. Poor Rainy won't talk to no one. She likes the money her girls pay too well. But then, don't we all? No money, no booze, no food. Look, lady, I just want to forget the whole thing."

Raven started to close the door.

"Look, I don't want to have you subpoenaed for you to go on the stand," Sally said, taking a more threatening approach. "It would be so much easier to talk to you right here. Surely you don't want to see an innocent person go to prison for something they didn't do."

"All right, you can come in, but I'm not talking in any court. I'm not happy about losing my meal ticket. The apartment will be up for rent as soon as the police say it's okay. I mind my own business and don't get involved with my tenants. I'm not grieving for them—except the money. Now come in."

Sally wanted to stay put right there on the porch. She hadn't exactly expected to be asked in, and she wasn't sure she wanted to go inside.

She stepped through the open doorway into what appeared to be a pleasant hall.

"Come in here and we can talk," Raven said. "It's no good on the porch. Too many eyes and too many ears." They proceeded through a door to their right. "This is my apartment. All these houses have been made into apartments. It pays the taxes and makes a living."

Sally sat down on a chesterfield that seemed clean. She hated to admit how good it felt and would have loved to kick off her shoes.

"You've done a really nice job of decorating in here," Sally said.

"Good, eh? I took a course in night school for decorating. It was just something to do. I buy a lot of items in old shops to give the place a new look."

"Well, I'm impressed." Sally kept moving her head, looking about to make it appear as though she was very interested. "I hardly know where to start. You say you're the owner of the house?"

"Yeah, it was originally my parents' home. They've been gone for a lot of years now, so I made the place a paying deal like all the rest of the houses in the neighbourhood. There's not enough cheap housing for people."

"I can understand that," Sally said. "We're having the same problems back east. Anyway, you certainly have a nice house. I understand from Clare Agnew that she came over personally to pay the rent on her daughter's apartment."

"Yeah, she did. Corey would have been all right, you know, if her ole lady had left her alone. They sure had some fights. She hated that friend of Corey's. Mrs. Agnew was a strong woman, if you know what I mean." She went on to confirm some of the things the neighbour had said.

"Was there anyone else around the house on the day of the murders?"

Raven hesitated before answering. "Well, there was the judge—and one other lady. She left right after the judge, a minute or two. She was quick, looked like she was in a hurry. I don't know who she was, and she could have been coming from another apartment. I didn't see her come in, you understand."

"Wait a minute," Sally said. "Do you mean there were two older ladies here?"

"No. I don't know that anyone was for sure in Corey's apartment. I only see who comes or goes down my front walk. Besides, the lady I mentioned walked too fast to be old."

"That means neither one of the ladies was Mrs. Agnew."

"Yes, ma'am. Well, maybe not. She might have been. I was watching my soap, so I really only saw the back of them as they left. I will say that Corey's mom wouldn't have killed her. She loved her daughter, no matter what she did."

Sally tried to figure out who all these women could be. Could one of them have been Judith Alves? No, that was ridiculous. She had to be at least forty-five, maybe fifty. Although she seemed to be involved with Uncle Hill in some way, she would be too smart to get involved in a murder. Her career was too important to her. On the other hand, there was a strange relationship between her and the judge. Maybe it was just a feeling on her part, only she was usually good at reading people.

Sally suddenly looked up, realizing she had been lost in thought. "I'm sorry, I was just thinking. I suppose the police have taped off the apartment and no one can go in."

"That's right."

"Would you mind if I went around to the apartments and asked if the last lady you saw was visiting any of the other people here?" Sally asked.

"They won't open their doors to a stranger. They won't like you."

"I understand. If you don't mind coming with me, that would be great." Sally smiled. "I have one more question. Do you have a key to the apartment where the girls lived, or did the cops take it?"

"Yes, they took the key." She smiled. "Although I still have a backup. The truth is, the police said I can't let in any reporters. They didn't say anything about someone like you."

They spent the next fifteen minutes very quickly moving from door to door. Each and every person who answered their doors seemed to provide an interesting experience. Sally slipped each one a twenty and hoped she wasn't being cheap. No one had entertained an older woman that afternoon.

Finally, near the end of the hall on the second floor, they stopped. It was obvious which apartment had been the murder scene. Sally recognized the black and yellow police tape trailing across the door.

"That was Corey's apartment," Raven said. "The police are done there."

"Raven, can you open the door? I'd like to see inside."

Raven didn't hesitate. She opened the door, the police tape fell away, and they walked in, leaving the door open a crack behind them.

"This is the first time I've been in here since the girls were killed," Raven said, sounding excited.

Sally was careful not to touch anything.

When Raven walked into the kitchen, she seemed upset to discover the dark brown stains on the floor, and the chalk lines where the bodies had been found.

CHAPTER EIGHT: THE MURDER SCENE

"Mrs. Agnew has already paid me rent for the next six months." Raven said. "She paid in advance so she wouldn't have to worry about things. I'm still waiting for her to tell me what she wants to do with all this furniture. Anyway, I'll have to offer cheap rent to get this apartment rented again. Who would want to live in a place where people were killed?"

Sally thought that was interesting. It seemed that judge wanted to keep this apartment for a while longer, at least six months. It didn't seem to matter to him that the girls had been killed here.

She and Raven left the apartment, closing the door behind them. Next, they approached the last apartment on the second floor, the one right next door to Corey's.

Even before they knocked, a young man appeared in the doorway.

"What where you doing in Corey's apartment, Mrs. Smith?" the man asked. "The police won't like that."

"It isn't Corey's apartment anymore, Tony, and it's none of your business." Raven almost sounded offended. "Besides, this here lady is a lawyer, so it's all right."

"You have no business going through her things," Tony said.

"I wasn't going through her things! I was just showing the apartment."

"I'm not a fool, Raven. You want to rent the apartment again." Tony's gaze went to Sally for the first time. "Who are you kidding, lady? You smell like press. Someone like you wouldn't want that apartment. So what are you after, a story?"

Sally didn't miss the vulgar expression on his face. This was the sleaze ball neighbour she'd been told about.

I'd better clean this up quickly, Sally thought. "Actually, I'm not here to rent the apartment. I'm an attorney representing the accused killer." She looked at him more closely. She had seen lots of guys like him and they weren't worth the time of day. "Did you know Corey?"

"Sure, I knew Corey as well as anyone," Tony said. "But no one really knew Corey, not even her old lady."

"Could I talk to you about her? I need to know as much as possible, anything that might be a help in court."

"Maybe. You can come in for a minute. Only you." He looked pointedly at Raven. "Not you."

"As if I would want to come into your den of iniquity," Raven said, shaking her head. To Sally, she added, "Be careful. He's insane. But suit yourself. If you go in there, I'm not responsible for what happens to you."

Raven turned back the way she had come.

"Mrs. Smith, I'll come down to see you again before I leave," Sally called after her.

Sally followed Tony into a little foyer. Just because she didn't like him didn't mean she couldn't look after herself. He might be a help. After all, she didn't think he was dangerous.

"You might as well come into the living room," Tony said. "Do you want a coffee?"

"No thanks." Sally sat in a chair. "The police think two older ladies went into that apartment the day the girls were killed, and also one man. You probably didn't see or hear much, huh? If you did see something unusual, I guess you would have told the police."

"You're kidding, right? Just say, for kicks, that I was home and it was quiet for most of the afternoon. Usually it was noisy, music blaring, lots of fights. Corey hated peace and quiet. She and her mom often went at it. They were dandies, two of a kind."

"How well did you know Corey and Joanna?"

"Just like I told the cops, I didn't. They weren't in my league. These babies had money and change bigtime. They weren't street girls, you know. I mean, they hit the streets the odd time when

CHAPTER EIGHT: THE MURDER SCENE

they were short and needed money, but mostly they had special friends who came to see them."

"Yet you say you didn't know them," Sally said, making a poker face as he stared at her. "That's funny, because I have a witness who will testify that you did know Corey."

"Joanna posed for me a few times. Corey? Never, not even for money. I take pictures, make movies, and mind my own business."

Sally hoped she didn't look surprised, but this seemed to lead back to the blackmail pictures she'd been told about. Was it possible Tony had taken them?

"Do you have your own dark room here in the apartment?" Sally asked.

"Sure. Most of the work I do is for my eyes only, although I sell a little bit. It's a living, see."

"I take it the police already talked to you about this."

"Sure, almost as soon as they found the girls dead. They talked to everyone in the place. Look, just for your information, I was as surprised as hell when I heard they were killed. Corey was asking for it, but she was the kind who always seemed to get away with everything. I can tell you right now: they weren't killed by some john."

"Did the police look around your apartment when they were here?"

"Not the first time, no warrant." He laughed. "They came back the next day with a warrant. They were very interested in my pictures."

Play it cool, she told herself. *Take it slow and smart.*

"Did they get the pictures or negatives of Corey and the judge?" she asked.

He smiled at her. "Smart cookie, ain't yah? There were no pictures to get. If I was the one to take them, you wouldn't expect me to keep them here. Lady, I'm not dumb."

"You didn't get arrested for other pictures you had?"

"Hell no, I moved everything as soon as I found out the girls were dead. I'm not crazy!"

Now Sally knew who the photographer had been. What to do about it, though, was another matter.

Don't do anything at this point, she thought. *Don't spook him. Leave that to Peter and his friends.*

"Okay, thanks." Sally stood up and started to walk back towards the door.

"Miss Attorney Lawyer Lady, I'll give you some free advice," Tony called after her. "If I were you, I would watch my back."

"I'll remember that." She left the apartment, not looking back.

Sally walked down the stairs and stopped outside Raven's apartment.

"Mrs. Smith?" she said, finding the door open. "Thank you again. I really appreciate your help. You've been very kind, and a lot of help to me."

Raven approached, looking wary. "Don't say I said anything, but that guy is into dirty pictures. He took some photos of the girls and the judge. He don't know I know. I saw them one day, but I'm not saying how. He's not a nice man."

Sally reached out to shake Raven's and left a fifty-dollar bill behind.

"Will I be needed to testify in court?" Raven asked. "The police told me there wouldn't be a court case."

Sally hesitated, surprised at that. "Probably not. Thanks again."

Forty minutes later, tired and worn out, she returned to Peter's house. She was surprised to learn that he hadn't come home yet. Almira offered her a drink to relax, but Sally explained that she was a teetotaller. She sat down to eat by herself, realizing how much she missed that man across the table from her. There was something very special about Peter.

She watched television for a while, and then went to bed. Tonight, with so much on her hand, she needed to feel close to the Lord. Sleep soon overtook her.

* * *

The next morning rolled in with a bright sun that seemed bigger than life over the flat, gorgeous prairie. Sally spent the first few hours working hard, making notes and putting ideas together, and before long she was tired again. This kind of mental strain was always so tough on a person.

She jumped in surprise as she heard the phone ring from another part of the house, echoing through the silence. Within seconds, Almira approached and stood in the doorway.

"The boss is on the telephone line for you, Miss Sally."

"Thank you, Almira." She put the phone to her ear. "Good morning, Peter. Don't you believe in taking Saturdays off?"

"Normally I keep my weekends free, unless there's something big going on, like this. How do you feel this morning?"

"Just fine. I slept in a little bit, which I never do."

"Good. That's what you needed." He cleared his throat. "Sally, I hope you don't mind, but I've hired someone to serve as your right hand gal until this case is wrapped up. There's a woman I know, Slipper McKinnon, who worked in the homicide department here for a few years before getting married and stepping away from the force. She still does undercover work now and then, as well as protection jobs."

Sally didn't say anything for a little while.

"Please don't say no, Sally," he continued. "I don't think there's anything to worry about yet, but I'm not stupid either. I always think it's better to be safe than sorry. Anyway, Slipper can use the money and I think you'll like her. She's tough but down to earth.

If your aunt didn't kill those girls, then someone else did, and that means there's a killer on the loose. Please take her with you everywhere you go. I think it's important, all right?"

Sally sighed. "Okay. I don't know why I would need a bodyguard, and I don't usually take threats too seriously. But my fiancé Mark always says that it's just part of the game we play." As she said this aloud, she started to get used to the idea. "I've called my uncle and set up an appointment with him at three o'clock. I was surprised that he's so willing to talk! And I have another couple of stops to make before seeing him."

"Great," Peter said. "Slipper will be along shortly. Be sure to take her with you."

Sally hung up as the line went dead. As she looked down at the phone, she thought of Peter's face.

What's wrong with me? she asked herself. *I love Mark.*

She was experiencing feelings she'd never had for Mark. Their relationship was like an old married couple, secure and trustworthy, like an old shoe.

With Peter, it was different.

CHAPTER NINE
A NEW SIDEKICK

About half-hour later, Almira came in through the door.
"Miss Sally, Slipper McKinnon is waiting in the other room. She says you're expecting her?" She said this with great dignity. "I know, Slipper. I think she was in love with the boss once, but she left him cold and hurting. She married someone else—a cop, of all people. It was for the better, though. You are far better for him."

Almira lifted her chin high, boastfully, having offered her opinion.

Peter certainly hadn't said anything like this to Sally. She expected Almira must be exaggerating.

Sally stood up just as her new bodyguard walked in. She immediately liked the look of Slipper.

"Hi," Sally said in greeting. "Please come in."

"Peter called me first thing this morning. He filled me in on your trouble." Slipper turned to smile at Almira. "Thanks, Almira. Can we talk alone?"

The housekeeper stepped back out into the hall.

"Almira doesn't like me too much," Slipper said as she walked in and sat next to the foldup table. "I guess you can tell."

"Yeah," Sally said. "Peter called a little while ago, but he didn't explain what an attractive lady I was getting."

"Don't worry. I'm not an old girlfriend or anything, no matter what Almira might have said." Slipper chuckled. "In fact, Peter and I are distantly related. Sixth cousins, I think, from the white side. He usually only admits to the Aboriginal side. The rest of us, he tolerates! The rebel in his soul, we say." She laughed a little louder, a hardy, robust sound. "Anyway, Peter says you're from Toronto. I worked my first job there, right downtown in Division 34. Do you know the area?"

Sally smiled. "No kidding! Yes, I know it. How long ago?"

"Let's see. I guess it was about fifteen years ago. Time has a way of passing too quickly, and suddenly you're left wondering where it went."

"You ever hear of a young detective, Mark Trotter?"

"Sure. Ladies men, if I remember right. Good looking, happy-go-lucky kind of guy. He was on fire for the job. I bet he made something of himself. A friend of yours?"

"Talk about coincidences. I'm engaged to marry him."

Slipper's forehead wrinkled. She didn't remember Mark being the marrying type. "Well, I guess they mellow with age. I'm not sure I would want a guy every other skirt wanted, though." She blushed. "Oh, sorry, I shouldn't have said that. Believe me, I'm no expert on men."

"Don't worry. I've heard the stories."

"Okay, Peter filled me in on what you are up to," Slipper said, getting down to business. "I'm here to see that nothing happens to you. Peter says you totally believe your aunt is innocent. I don't suppose I need to say it, but you have your job cut out for you. Are you planning on going out today? You're quite hot at the moment."

"I have an appointment this afternoon, then I'm going to my uncle's condo later," Sally said. "I'll take you with me, if you don't mind. Just make sure, when we see the judge, that you don't say anything about Peter. I don't want him to know where I'm staying."

Slipper nodded. "Of course. I'm just here to help you, and your aunt. I want to know the truth."

That made Sally feel better. "Okay. I'm glad to have you along. In fact, if you're ready, we might as well go right away."

"Do you mind if I drive? I have my own car. I know its temperament and what it can do."

"Sure, that will be great." She wasn't sure she could keep her mind on the road anyway, with everything that was going on.

On their way out, Almira stood at the front door with a huge bouquet of fresh flowers and an empty vase.

"From our garden," she said. "Please take these to your aunt. Maybe they will cheer her up. And Miss Sally, please tell her that we all know she didn't do what they say, and that we're praying for her."

Sally took them, even though she didn't think the guards would let her aunt have them. "Thanks, Almira. I will. And as for the prayer, she's going to need all she can get. That is very kind, thank you."

Slipper passed right by Almira, giving the housekeeper a little glare.

Once in the car, they made their way to the highway. Slipper took her time, watching for any other vehicles that might be following them. She had a good feel for menace and danger, but fortunately she didn't find anything suspicious.

"I like your name," Sally said. "I've never heard anything like it."

"That's just my dad's sense of humour. My mom got pregnant really late in life, so I guess it was a bit of a slipup. He always says he could have called me Slipup, so I shouldn't complain." She laughed again, tossing her red-blond hair.

Sally already liked her very much. The two women were about the same age and height, though Slipper must have been a little younger.

"Your husband doesn't mind you doing this kind of job?" Sally asked.

"Hell yes. He hates it. We have two teenagers in university, though, so the extra money comes in handy. He's with the police department and doesn't seem to care if he gets killed, as long as the kids still have a mother. Some reasoning, eh? Anyway, as cops we know what we're signing up for. I have to tell you, leaving full-time police work was one of the most difficult decisions I've ever had to make. I loved being a cop."

"I can relate. Mark loves being in the force, so I accept that. I try not to worry about him, but it's not easy." She paused, turning to her plans for the day. "First I need to do some shopping. When I came here, I wasn't planning to stay so long or do anything special. I just need to find a small boutique around here."

"You're the boss!" Slipper said. "So does this mean you and Peter are going someplace special? You can tell me to mind my own business, if you like."

"He mentioned something about going out for dinner. I admit, I've come to like Peter too much, and it's a problem. I keep telling myself that I love Mark, but Peter is so caring. Mark takes me for granted sometimes. We might as well have been married for years. I don't even know how it happened."

Tell me about it, Slipper wanted to say. She had her own problems.

Just then, Sally's eye caught sight of a nice-looking boutique shop that would fill the bill nicely. "There! That store looks perfect. Can you pull the car up?"

Slipper stopped the car and locked the doors as they walked inside. Slipper went in first and gave a quick look around to make sure everything was okay. She still didn't know who their enemy was, which meant she had to watch out for anything that could mean trouble.

"Good afternoon," a shopkeeper said as Sally entered. "May I help you?"

"Maybe," said Sally. "Do you mind if I look around for just a few minutes?"

"Of course not, my dear." She moved a few feet away, allowing Sally and Slipper to browse the fashions on display.

"Okay, I'm leaving you to it," Slipper said. "I would feel better if I could keep my eye on the street outside. You're fine in here."

Slipper walked outside and looked up and down the street. It was difficult when she didn't know what she was really looking for. There had been no other people in the store, though, and she was thankful for that.

In the small change room, Sally stood back and looked at one of the best outfits in the mirror. She turned around a couple of times, finding that it was both smart and well-tailored. The outfit was a tomato-red suit, with a skirt featuring tiny box pleats sewn down the hipline. It was shorter than anything Sally had ever worn, yet very comfortable.

She then decided to try on another suit of the same material, black crepe wool, which was very elegant with slight, beaded lapels. The skirt was long with a very high slit, and she had never worn anything like it. Accompanying this was a green satin camisole.

Wow, she thought as she turned in front of the mirror. *This number is a knockout!*

The third option was a butter yellow jumpsuit, both plain yet rich-looking. The colour was stunning. It came with a long, sheer scarf. Sally wasn't sure what to do with it; she tried it several ways, each position better than the last.

She walked out of the change room exactly fifteen minutes later, planning to purchase all three selections. The saleswoman clipped off the tags off the red suit so Sally could wear it out of the store.

Sally hadn't felt this good for some time. She actually felt younger, and also a little bit foolish. She hoped this wasn't too dressy for the calls she still had to make.

"You look smashing," Slipper said when Sally walked outside.

If Peter lets this one get away, he's crazy, the bodyguard thought. How many young women could get away with a bright red suit like that? Now, she just needed to keep her from being killed! Peter seemed certain that someone wanted Sally out of the way. Their enemies dared not let her take the case to court.

Soon, they were moving once again.

"I'm going to enjoy having someone to drive around," Sally commented. "This way, I can concentrate on what I have to do today—and I plan to keep a tight schedule. Next, we need to go see my aunt. I want her to know that she isn't alone or forgotten. I'm only planning to stay for a few minutes."

Slipper headed for the courthouse, all the while thinking about what she would have to do to stay close and make sure they both stayed out of harm's way. Sometimes that would be easy, other times not so easy. It all depended on who wanted to take her out and how badly.

Sally looked up as they entered the parking lot and stopped right in her uncle's reserved spot. She noticed that a security guard was already on the way over.

Great, this is all I need, Sally thought.

As he got closer, Sally saw that she recognized this guard from yesterday. Hopefully he would recognize her, too.

"You know, no matter what anyone says, this is one of those times when it would be nice to be a man," Sally said. "A man probably wouldn't be treated this way."

Slipper sighed. "Leave him to me. I'll handle it."

The guard came right up to the window. Slipper lowered the glass.

"Good afternoon, Ms. Cameron," the man said, looking right past Slipper. "I just wanted you to know that you're more than welcome anytime to use your uncle's parking spot. He informed us this morning that you might park here. By the way, welcome to Regina. I hope you enjoy your holiday."

"Thanks, that's much appreciated." Sally smiled, although her heart wasn't in it.

Holiday! Yeah right, she thought as the guard moved off.

"That must be what my uncle is telling people. That I'm on holiday," Sally said to Slipper. "Very interesting, don't you think? He thinks I'm the enemy at the moment, and I may well be. But I'm not going to cooperate with him, no matter what he says."

Slipper shrugged. "You might be right, but you just got the royal treatment."

"We'll see."

They got out of the car, Sally carrying the bouquet of handpicked flowers from Almira's garden. She hoped the guards would let her give them to her aunt. One never could be sure what they would allow.

Poor Slipper was right on her heels, her eyes scanning the area as they approached the door.

Once inside, they made their way along the hall. A few minutes later, they were on their way into her aunt's luxury cell.

"There's not enough chairs for you," Sally said, touching Slipper's arm.

"I'll just wait outside. Holler if you want me."

Sally noticed that her aunt looked right up as Sally walked toward her. That was a good sign.

"Sally dear, I wasn't sure if you would come today. I'm so glad you did. I have a few things to tell you."

"Why wouldn't I come to see you? Well, here I am, with some lovely flowers from the garden of a friend."

Lisa smiled. "Do you think we could put them in water to keep them as long as possible?"

"I'll get some water from the sink." Sally stepped into the little bathroom and poured some water into the empty vase. She returned in a minute.

Lisa put the flowers under her nose, then set them down again on the table.

"Now tell me, what did you want to talk about?" Sally asked.

"My husband, dear. He's getting very difficult and he doesn't want you here."

"Has he been to see you since yesterday?" One look at her aunt's concern told Sally that this was going to take longer than planned. Sally pulled up a chair and sat down.

"No, my dear, but he was on the phone. We talked about this place for a few minutes, and then I told him I didn't kill the girls. Sally, he became very upset with me. Hill says I'm crazy and that I just don't remember doing it."

"We certainly agree you're not crazy, Aunt Lisa."

"Hill says he has proof that I killed the girls, that someone was at the apartment and saw me shoot them before passing out. He says the prosecution has this person as a witness. The dreadful thing is, he might be right. I really don't remember what happened, and I've tried so hard. I only remember when I woke up on the floor. I thought I was alone, until Hill got there. Now I'm not so sure."

Sally kept herself still, trying not to get angry. What should she say to her aunt? She didn't want to come right out and condemn her Uncle.

CHAPTER NINE: A NEW SIDEKICK

"Aunt Lisa, I couldn't agree more about the fact that there was someone else in that apartment besides you. The only difference is, I believe that person is the killer." In this case, Sally felt that abruptness was better than kindness. "Aunt Lisa, remember that were going to leave this to me. You must not talk to anyone, even Uncle hill, not even about the weather. Even if he does mean well, we're trying to save your life, not his."

Lisa uttered a great sigh. "That wasn't the worst part of it, you know."

"All right, Aunt Lisa, what was the worst part?"

"Hill insisted that I tell you to go home, that I take the advice Ben Purveys and hire his son as my lawyer. I told him no, straight out, since you're my attorney and I already signed a paper that says so." She looked down at the toes of her shoes as a tear trickled down her face. "He says you can't be my lawyer, because I'm mentally unfit and anything I signed is no good. He said he can prove that, too."

"He did, did he? Well, we'll see about that. This is ridiculous." Sally's mind went into lawyer mode. "He won't get away with this. Aunt Lisa, don't you dare believe that for one minute. I will find a proper doctor to examine you and prove him wrong."

Sally spent another half-hour assuring her aunt that everything was going to be all right. After they said their goodbye, she thought it was more important than ever that she talk to her uncle. At least she seemed to have him worried. Or was it the other way around?

When they left the building and approached the car, Slipper put her hand on Sally's arm to stop her.

"What's the matter?" Sally asked.

"Good question. It's probably just my imagination working overtime. Stay here a minute." Slipper walked to their car, noticing that there were now cars parked on either side of it. She then lay right on the ground and looked under the car, seeing nothing there that should worry her.

Yet she *was* worried.

Sally had walked towards the car, standing at the rear of the vehicle. What in the world was Slipper doing?

"Don't come any closer, Sally. This probably sounds silly, but I'm going to call the police and have them check it out before we get inside."

Slipper thought she was going to be unpopular tonight if they didn't find anything. Every once in a while, it was like a little person sat on her shoulder and shouted warnings to her. Many times it had saved her life when she was undercover.

Right at that moment, a couple of reporters noticed Sally standing alone in the parking lot and started towards her. Sally tried to get away, moving closer to Slipper.

"Some reporters are heading over," Sally said. "Can we please get out of here?"

"I don't think so. I have a funny feeling about the car. Better to face a few reporters than end up dead."

"What sort of funny feeling? What do you mean, dead?"

"I'm not sure I can explain. Sometimes I get little warning feelings—and those feelings are usually right."

Sally wasn't sure what to think. "There must be something we can do."

"Just trust me." Slipper touched her arm. "Let's move back a ways, to be on the safe side."

The reporters were getting close now.

"Look, everyone, just stay away from that car for a minute," Slipper called to them. "I think there might be something in it that could blow up." From their expressions, she obviously didn't believe her. "Please guys, I'm serious."

Well, she had warned them. It was their own fault now if they got hurt.

Slipper punched some numbers into her phone and spoke to the police for a few minutes. When she done, she lowered her hand.

"A couple of police cars will be right here," she said. "Sorry, everyone."

"Are you a cop?" one the reporters asked. "And whose car is it?"

"It's mine." Slipper was happy they were suddenly more interested in the car than in Sally.

"What makes you think there is a bomb in the car?" asked another reporter with a camera in hand. "Are you with Ms. Cameron? Do you think the bomb is meant for her?"

The first reporter stepped closer. "Ms. Cameron, is it true your aunt is mentally unstable? Is your family going to use this as a cover-up?"

Sally stepped behind Slipper as two patrol cars pulled up. Four policemen walked up, keeping a wary eye on the reporters.

"Hi, Slipper," one cop said. "What's up?"

"Hi guys. I think something is wrong with my car. I'm afraid to open the door in case it goes up."

"Are you serious? You mean like a bomb or something? What are you into, and why the reporters?"

"It's a long story. Will one of you give it good check? I looked under and didn't see anything, but I can't be sure. Please be careful."

The cop turned to the others. "Carl, you and Jake check under her."

A couple of guys hit the ground and studied the bottom of the car while someone else poked at the door with his nightstick.

"I'm going to open the door now," he said. "I need everyone to get back and out of the way."

Even the other cops moved back as the first cop opened the door and jumped back, just in case. One reporter stepped back, but the other stood his ground, too nosy for his own good. The whole thing struck Sally as a bit funny, but she dared not laugh. Nerves must be getting to them. Surely no one wanted her dead.

About two minutes later, it seemed the danger had passed.

"I'm going to check inside the car now," said the same cop who had opened the door.

Just as he was getting close, a trail of smoke rose from inside the car. It started with a little puff, then a sizzle, and then the vehicle exploded, tumbling everyone away in a huge blast. The cars on either side had caught fire, too, and they were all burning at the same time, hurling black smoke into the air.

As Sally's head cleared, she saw that the reporters were lying on the cement, having been thrown backward.

Before she could think, Slipper threw herself protectively in front of her.

"I'm fine, thanks," Sally said. "Slipper, you all right? I'm not sure about the others. I could have been killed! I can't believe this."

"Well, I told them to stand back." Slipper looked down at herself. "I'm dusty and dirty, but no broken bones. We're lucky we didn't get into that car or we'd be toast. Sally, someone wants you dead, real bad. No one can do this and get away with it! But whoever did it isn't smart. Now the police will get involved."

"Slipper, you saved my life." Sally's voice conveyed shock and terror. She couldn't believe what she was seeing right in front of her eyes. The air shimmered from the heat and the fire. "I hope those other two cars have insurance!"

Slipper ignored that last comment. "I'm just glad you're all right."

The reporter with the camera stumbled to his feet and started snapping photos of the carnage.

"The fire department is on the way," one of the cops spoke.

Slipper nodded. "Let's get you inside, Sally. I don't like it out here."

It seemed everyone was all right. She thought one of those reporters might have a broken arm, and one of the cops had burns to his arm and the side of his face, but ambulances would be on their way to look after them.

The next hour was pure bedlam with the police, firefighters, and paramedics—and of course there were lots of question. Sally and Slipper gave their statements.

Sally didn't even want to think about what the media was going to show on the evening news. She just let Slipper do all the talking.

Sometime later, she sat inside the front door of someone's office at the courthouse. No one seemed to be very interested in her anymore, with all the activity outside.

Once the scene had calmed down, Slipper had a policeman take them back to the station. From there, Slipper managed to rent another car. It would take them a while to settle their nerves, so Slipper drove them to a nearby park.

"I owe you a car, Slipper, and my life. How can I repay that?" They hugged and cried some more.

"This isn't your fault. Besides, my car was old. Now I have an excuse to buy a new one."

Sally knew she owed her life to Slipper, so she would make sure Slipper got a new car at her expense.

When she talked to Peter on the phone, he insisted that they head home, but she refused. More than ever, she had to prove that she wouldn't be frightened away. The truth was, she was scared silly. She didn't tell him that, though.

They had to find out who had done this.

CHAPTER TEN
MEETING BEN PURVEYS

They spent the next twenty minutes making their way back to her uncle's condo. Once they arrived, the front of the building was teeming with reporters, as usual. Sally explained to Slipper how to get in the back door and to the freight elevator.

It didn't take long before they were inside and Sally was standing with her back against the elevator's wall as they rode up. She only breathed a sigh of relief when the door opened again and she walked out.

Slipper smiled. "Don't like elevators?"

"No. To be honest, I walk up and down whenever possible."

"I'll wait out here in the hall if you want."

"Thanks. It's true that he may talk more freely if I'm alone, but I feel like I need you close by, after everything that's happened," Sally said. "I hate to admit how little I trust this man. Sorry, I'm normally not such a coward."

Sally tapped the brass knocker as Slipper leaned against the wall, giving her the thumbs-up sign. They were both a little jittery.

"Oh Sally, I was so afraid you wouldn't be coming back," Anna said when she answered the door. She gave Sally a big hug. "I'm sure you can use me in some way to help us all out of this terrible

CHAPTER TEN: MEETING BEN PURVEYS

situation." Then, letting Sally out of her arms, she pointed to Slipper. "Who's that?"

"Anna works for my uncle and aunt," Sally said to Slipper. She turned back to the housekeeper. "This is Slipper, a good friend."

"Hi," Slipper said, smiling at the woman despite her critical look.

"Follow me." Anna turned, ignoring the stranger. "Your uncle is waiting."

"Anna, do you think Aunt Lisa killed the two girls?" Sally asked as they entered the apartment.

We need Sally to go home, Anna thought as she stopped and turned. *She just doesn't understand the problem.*

Sally stared right at her, able to see the struggle going on inside the woman. She knew Anna had always been very fond of her aunt.

"I don't know," Anna said. "Sally, you must be able to help her and the judge. The judge says there are wonderful places for people who have money and aren't quite right in the mind. That would give us all such a perfect solution. We're all so concerned. What's going to happen to us all?"

"Thanks, Anna. I'll keep that in mind."

Sally left the housekeeper standing in the foyer and carried on into the sitting room with Slipper at her side.

"Keep calm and don't get upset," Slipper said to her. "After all, she's only the hired help. What does she know? Maybe your uncle will accept me if you say I'm your secretary, not a bodyguard. That would allow me to make notes if I hear something important. And I don't have to say anything."

"That's perfect. I'll say that I hired you from an old friend. Maybe it's better you are in the room."

They were interrupted as her uncle entered the room from his den. He looked tall and handsome.

"Sally, my dear, it's so good to see you again," her uncle said.

"You too, Uncle Hill." She kissed his cheek and immediately noticed another gentleman she didn't know, sitting in a large chair by the gas fireplace. "I'm sorry we're a little late. A few things came up." She indicated her friend. "Uncle, this is Slipper, an old friend. As you have someone here, too, I guess you won't mind that I brought one."

Slipper stepped forward, quite surprised. She knew the other man in the room, even though it was obvious that Sally didn't. Clearly, her uncle had been ready for this visit. She wanted to warn Sally, but she had no idea how to do that.

Slipper just nodded to the man in recognition, not sure what more to do. He nodded back, scrutinizing her.

This judge is far too smart for his own good, Slipper thought. *Poor Sally has no idea what she's up against.*

She immediately recognized the judge, too, from being in his court a few times. He was a very handsome man.

"It's nice to meet you, Your Honour." Slipper shook his hand. "Sally has told me so many wonderful things about the times she spent with you over the years."

Sally noticed that the stranger in the comfortable chair looked right at home. She also noticed that Slipper seemed to know more than she did. Did that mean this man knew Slipper was a cop?

The stranger was a man in his early sixties. The dye in his greying hair made him look a little younger, but he was quite sophisticated. She was usually good with first impressions.

Suddenly, Sally realized who he was. It was the father of her school chum, Donald. He looked like Don—or maybe it was the other way around. If things had gone differently, he could have been her father-in-law. Now, that was funny! She remembered Don saying once that his father was her uncle's lawyer.

CHAPTER TEN: MEETING BEN PURVEYS

Slipper had sat in a chair slightly to the side of this man she knew only too well.

"Sally, dear, excuse me," Uncle Hill said. "You seem miles away. This is a very special old friend of mine, Ben Purveys. We've been friends for years."

"How do you do?" Sally said. "I guess we haven't met, although I know a bit about you, Mr. Purveys." She let that sink in for a minute, causing him some speculation. "I dated your son for a while back in university."

Ben kept a neutral expression. "That would have been the University of Toronto, I gather?"

She nodded. "I admit that seems a hundred years ago now. Anyway, this is my friend Slipper, an ex-cop. She's working as my secretary on this trip."

Sally worried about questioning her uncle with the lawyer in the room. Maybe that was why he was here, to stop her in case she asked the wrong questions.

"Slipper and I have met," Ben said, turning to her. "I remember you from the force. I'm surprised you left. I'm not sure playing secretary is your thing."

"You have a good memory, Mr. Purveys," Slipper said. She caught that he had used the word *playing*. "I've known Sally for years, so when she needed help I was only too glad to oblige. I know people in high places, so I can help her get appointments and so on. I'm sure you understand."

"It isn't often I am surprised, young lady," Ben replied, then shifted to address both women. "Actually, you've both surprised me. I must say, Ms. Cameron, it's strange that Donald never mentioned having such a beautiful girlfriend. But I'm pleased to meet you."

Ben stood up and approached, shaking Sally's hand. He held it a little longer than necessary.

"Ms. Cameron—may I call you Sally?—I'm sure this whole situation has been a terrible shock to you. I remember my last visit here, just a couple of weeks ago, when your aunt was behaving most peculiar. Your uncle explained that she hadn't been well for about six months. I'm very concerned."

Sally sighed. "Well, I see nothing whatsoever wrong with my aunt. I'm on her side."

"I have to say, my dear, there are no sides here," Ben said. "Wherever you heard that, it's wrong. We're all family and friends. Our only interest is in seeing that your aunt is looked after."

"Actually, I've spoken to Aunt Lisa about this," said Sally. "She wants me to represent her in court. I've agreed, and as far as I'm concerned it's all settled. I see nothing wrong with her mental capacity. I have a doctor who will confirm this."

She quickly noted the surprised look on both their faces. It wasn't a lie. No doubt Peter could find a doctor.

"You're wrong, my dear," Ben insisted. "Lisa isn't well. One minute she wants one thing, and the next another. You cannot depend on what she says. Her mind comes and goes. Sometimes it's very reasonable, other times she seems totally gone. I've had a doctor see her several times and he'll vouch for this. You haven't been with her long enough to find out the truth. I beg of you not to interfere. Your uncle and I know what's best for your aunt."

Sally frowned at him. "I've spent several hours with Aunt Lisa since I've been here. I don't find her to be at all unwell."

"Come, my dear, you must realize she's not—"

Sally ignored him. "One more question, Mr. Purveys. Do you believe my aunt killed those two girls?"

"Yes, I absolutely do! That's exactly why she needs my help. I'll arrange the very best plea bargain we can get. There will be no trial. On the other hand, with your persistence, you may try to prove her innocence and get her locked up for the rest of her life. If you were in your aunt's shoes, who would you rely on?"

"Wow!" Sally almost laughed. "Now that's hard one. Let me see… a prison or an insane asylum. What a decision to make—"

"Sally, you have this all wrong," said Uncle Hill. "Mount Merry Meadow isn't an asylum at all." He hesitated. "It's more like a hotel. I've been there to see it for myself, and it's a fine place. They'll look after her and she'll get the best care possible."

"Sorry, Uncle, it's still a prison. My aunt did not kill those girls." Sally turned to look her uncle right in the eye. "I am her lawyer now, and I'm going to prove she didn't do it. I only need to establish reasonable doubt. Believe me, I already have that."

Ben stepped between them. "Hill, please, I think you're getting far too personal here. Sally, if I may, maybe you would do better to come back another time. You're both under a great deal of strain and need to look at this situation from a different viewpoint."

"Okay, Uncle Hill, for once the man is right," Sally said, still seething. "I'll be in touch."

Sally needed to get out of there before she exploded. She walked away, Slipper and the men following behind. She would have given anything to leave a bug in the room, but it wasn't possible.

"It was interesting to have met you, Mr. Purveys," Sally said when they got to the door. "At least I know what to expect now, and it doesn't bother me one bit." She shook his hand. "You can count on seeing me in court. Say hello to Donald for me."

Sally didn't say goodbye. She just walked out, praying she wouldn't lose her temper as she trudged down the hallway. She was filled with deep anger, so much of it that she could scream.

She resolved never to come back here as long as she lived. She hoped her aunt never had to, either.

"No elevator this time, Slipper," she called over her shoulder. "I have to walk off the steam. I'm using the stairs."

She took her time going down the stairwell, counting each step as she descended flight after flight. Once they got down to the foyer, she turned and saw that Slipper wasn't even breathing heavily.

"You're not out of breath?" she asked.

Slipper shrugged. "Neither are you. I exercise every day. It's important, since I only work part-time." They turned and walked toward the back entrance. "Sally, that uncle of yours is quite something. I'm glad I'm not in your shoes. And I can tell you one thing about Ben Purveys—he'll do everything he can think of to prove you wrong. You've made a very serious enemy."

"He's not the first," Sally said. "You have no idea how difficult it is to fight for what a woman believes in. This world still belongs to the men."

* * *

When they arrived back at Peter's house, they found a nice room for Slipper to relax. Afterward Sally lay down in bed and dozed for an hour. Then she woke up, showered, and decided to wear one of the other outfits she'd purchased. The one she had worn all day had been through too much.

She felt very comfortable that evening as she and Slipper made their way back to the city. Peter had given them the address of a hotel where they were to meet. Slipper dropped her off at the front entrance, just as Peter was walking up from the parking lot. Slipper drove them, leaving them alone for the evening.

"Sally, you look wonderful," he said, pleasure written all over his face. "Marvellous."

"Thank you, kind sir."

"Have you been to see your uncle today?"

"Yes. But I'm going to try forgetting everything he said and just enjoy myself tonight. I'm famished. I've been so busy that I didn't get any lunch, not even a coffee. Poor Slipper! She's going to have to remind me to eat from now on. She must be starving, too."

He put his hand in hers and they walked back into the hotel, stepping into the lovely restaurant next to the lobby. The host brought them to a table with large leafy plants on each side, giving them some privacy. A large stage stood off to the side. It seemed there was to be some sort of dinner theatre later on.

"I hate being crowded," he said, looking right into her lovely eyes.

The waiter appeared almost immediately to explain that they could help themselves to the buffet. Peter gave him their drink orders.

"I know you don't drink alcohol," Peter said. "But just wait until you taste what I ordered for you. I'm sure you'll enjoy it very much. No alcohol, just six different squeezed juices whipped together with soda."

When the waiter returned with the drinks, Sally took a sip and it was just as he had said—frothy and wonderful.

She smiled at him, licking away the foam from her lips. "I've never tasted anything like it. It's delicious. Did you invent this?"

Together, they walked to the buffet and helped themselves to wonderfully fresh food. Sally ate like a pig and enjoyed every bite. For dessert, they could choose from several amazing options. She settled for a strawberry shortcake smothered in chocolate and whipped cream.

Finally, their table was cleaned off. The waiter left behind a thermos of coffee.

"Everything tasted superb," Sally said. "Thank you, Peter."

Peter slipped his arm around her shoulders as they watched the dinner theatre. She knew right that instant that she should have moved away, but she didn't. She refused to think about Mark and what was the right thing to do. Peter knew she was engaged, but maybe he didn't care. Maybe he was just looking for a short affair. If so, that wasn't her thing. He would be in for a surprise.

The show was a comedy, and Sally was surprised to even recognize some of the stars. She laughed several times and thoroughly enjoyed herself.

To top off the evening, Peter had an interview with the stars afterward, which she sat in on. She came away with three autographs she would cherish for some time to come.

On the way home, they stopped for another coffee, only returning to the house at two-thirty in the morning. They stepped out of the car in the midst of a beautiful night. Together, they walked for a while along the garden path. They ended up under a huge shade tree and exchanged several kisses. Sally had to admit, Peter was nothing like Mark; he was far more passionate.

She wished she could stay in this moment forever. It had to be the atmosphere! She hated to admit that Peter was more romantic than Mark had ever been. In a way, Mark hadn't ever needed to win her; he'd had so many girls chasing him.

Eventually, Peter walked her back to the house.

"Good night, Sally," Peter said, then returned to his bedroom.

Sally saw no one about and made her way along the hallway to her own room.

CHAPTER ELEVEN
CONFUSION

As another morning dawned, Peter suggested that they attend the church he went to, allowing Sally to discover that he was a Christian, something she had been hoping would happen for Mark. After the benediction, they left and went to lunch at a lovely little restaurant. They spent the afternoon touring the city, including a visit to the Saskatchewan Museum of Natural History. They also saw the Royal Canadian Mounted Police Historical Museum, and finally the Norman Mackenzie Art Gallery, a place close to her heart as she loved to paint.

Although Peter made no move to touch her today, she felt his love with every gesture.

When Monday morning arrived, she showered, dressed, and prayed for God's guidance before making her way to Almira's kitchen. There she found Peter waiting for her. They exchanged some small talk, then looked after their empty stomachs. Almira had prepared an excellent breakfast for the day ahead.

While waiting for Slipper to arrive, Sally realized that it was strange for Peter not to have left yet.

"I'm expecting my brother, although I thought he would have been here an hour ago," Peter explained. "Something must have detained him. Sometimes our best plans don't work out, and I have to make myself accept that."

Then, as though by clockwork, she looked toward the front hall, hearing some noise on the driveway. Was it Slipper? She was about to get up from her chair when Almira entered the sitting room with a man—presumably Peter's brother. He and Peter greeted one another by patting each other on the back.

"Do you have that little item I wanted?" Peter asked.

"Normally I would just hand it over without saying anything," he said. "Well, maybe a little something." He hesitated, eyeing Sally. "You have such a beautiful friend!"

Peter smiled. "Yes. Well, she might be too pretty for me to introduce to my single brother who likes women a little too well. I'm no fool. Besides, if you look carefully you'll see that she's engaged. To a very rich man, no less. That leaves you right out in the cold."

Sally listened to their banter without really understanding their relationship.

"Now wait a minute," his brother said. "I'm only a half-brother on your white side, if you please." He laughed. "Anyway, I think I should get an introduction!"

"Right. But did you bring that information I wanted?"

"Yes. Does this have to be so business-like, little brother?" He handed him a small cassette tape. "I must be going. Too bad you won't let me meet the beautiful lady. Maybe another time." He smiled at Sally, then walked out of the house as quickly as he'd come in.

Sally was confused from trying to follow their conversation. That man had looked nothing like Peter, despite being his half-brother.

"Here's the tape of everything that was said in your uncle's apartment on Saturday. It's a good thing you recorded it!" Peter hesitated. "Nevertheless, we can't use it in court, as it was recorded illegally. It may be some help, though. I suggest you listen to it, take notes, and then flush it down the toilet. And be careful how you use the information."

"Thank you, Peter. I can't tell you how important this is to me."

"I'll see you tonight." He smiled and walked away.

Slipper arrived a short time later and they shared a few laughs, talking like old friends about how they'd spent their Sundays. Finally, after Sally explained what she had planned for the rest of the day, they left the house with Slipper driving.

They soon arrived at the courthouse. Slipper once again pulled the car into Sally's uncle's parking space, taking note of the blackened pavement. It sent an ominous chill through both women.

As they walked through the corridor inside, a funny feeling came over Sally that she couldn't explain. A chill ran straight down her back. She shivered, trying to ignore it. Maybe the temperature was just a bit too cool in here.

That's when Sally looked up and saw Clare Agnew walking toward them.

"Here comes Clare," Sally whispered. "I wonder if she was watching for us."

Sally felt the air around them fill with apprehension as Clare drew nearer, taking her time to reach them.

"What a lovely surprise," Clare said when they were standing right in front of each other. "I was actually going to call and see if you would come and talk for a bit today. I guess you're on your way to see Lisa. I have a few spare minutes. Could we talk first?" She made eye contact with Slipper. "I don't believe we've met before. I understand you used to work for the police department? Judge Cameron tells me you still do odd jobs for the police. Sally's fortunate to have such a good friend." Clare looked down at her wristwatch, then looked up, abruptly changing the subject. "Sally, do you mind if I get right to the point? I've had a long talk with the judge and we've tried every way we can think of to settle this thing your way. I'm afraid it's just impossible. Your uncle really cares about you and has asked me to talk to you. He's hoping I can convince you to go home and leave this in our hands."

Sally bristled. "You're right, Clare, that's right to the point. I can't tell you how much I want to go home. I would give anything if I could just get on a plane and turn the clock back, let me see… several years. You see, the problem is we can't go back. We can't fix the mistakes that have been made unless we make decisions to bring about a better tomorrow. These mistakes have been years in the making."

Clare frowned, hoping she would be successful at keeping Sally talking for a while longer. Then everything would be all right, and they would have won.

"Clare, I don't believe there is a family anywhere that doesn't have skeletons in their closet. They eventually come out—yesterday, today, or tomorrow. Well, I guess some families are lucky and never have to reveal them. Mind you, I'm not saying that's good. Unfortunately for the Camerons, we're in the midst of opening that closet door, and I have no idea what's going to emerge. I do believe we're all strong enough to handle whatever it is. I also hope we all become closer as a family. And I suppose you're a Cameron too, for all intents and purposes. I'm sorry I never knew Corey." Sally sighed. "Who knows? We might have been friends had this situation been handled differently. But it sounds to me like Corey never had a chance. Maybe you have to take some responsibility for that."

"You have no idea what you're talking about," Clare snapped back, her voice wavering. "You're just a young thing with your whole life ahead of you. I would get on my knees and beg if I thought it would get you out of our lives. Is there any way, anything, I can say to get you to leave us alone?"

Sally shook her head. "You know as well as I do that it's not going to happen. I will defend my aunt against these murder charges, and I'll call anyone to the stand if I have to—you, Judith, everyone in the courthouse if I have to."

The two women stared at each other. Something was wrong. As sure as she was standing there, Clare wasn't the least bit afraid. Why? That was the question.

What does she know that I don't? Sally wondered.

"Ms Cameron…" Clare looked at her watch again and smiled. "I've said all I intend to say today. Ben Purveys is my attorney, though, and you may talk to him if you wish. He said I wasn't to talk to you at all from this moment on. He also told me to tell you we'll file harassment charges against you if you persist in coming after me."

"Clare, you're the one who asked me to talk, remember? I was just on my way to see my aunt."

Sally took a deep breath. What was going on? She dared not look at Slipper, yet she really wanted her friend's input.

Clare just walked away. Sally looked at Slipper and shrugged her shoulders.

"I'm too upset to go see my aunt right now," Sally said. "We can come back tonight. I just want out of this place or I'll start screaming. I'm so angry. What a woman!"

Slipper was having trouble keeping up with Sally as she wasted no time leaving.

"Sally, we need to talk."

"Let's get in the car first. I have to make a phone call. Just have some patience with me for a minute." She paused. "It was like Clare had some big secret I knew nothing about, and that does worry me."

Once they were in the car, Slipper drove far enough away that none of the reporters standing around the front entrance even noticed them.

"Where are we going?" Slipper asked.

"Wascana Park. I need to sit in peace on a park bench, do some thinking, and call my father. Then we can go back and see my aunt."

"All right, I can go along with that."

Only a few minutes later, they were sitting on a park bench.

"Sally, I'm not interested in listening in on your call to your father, but I can't leave your side."

"Right. So just plug your ears. It will be short—and not sweet."

Sally took her cell phone from her purse, dialled her father's number, and waited for him to answer.

"Sally, at last," he said when he picked up. "I've been going crazy with calls from Hill about you. I'm in my office, alone for a bit, but I'm due back in court in fifteen minutes. Now, where are you staying and why in the world don't you answer your phone? My brother is beside himself. He says you're making more problems for them. You must come home right now."

"First of all, Dad, there's something very peculiar going on here and I don't believe there's anything wrong with Aunt Lisa. I know what Uncle Hill is saying, but I don't agree with him."

"Sally, for goodness sake, use your head. Your uncle knows your aunt far better than you do. You have to stop this nonsense and come home immediately. Look, I have to go. I'll expect you to call when you land back in Toronto later this evening."

The line went dead and Sally sat there, staring at the small phone in her hand.

She put through another call, and after listening to the answering machine realized that Mark wasn't back yet from his undercover job. She left a short message, explaining that he should call when he returned.

All this had done was get her even more upset. She had known her father would be touchy, but that call had been ridiculous. This was a man who dealt in life and death decisions. Shouldn't she have been able to expect him to understand her point of view?

No, she wasn't going there.

"Slipper, I'm being tossed in so many different directions. My biggest fear, and one I can't get out of my brain, is the fact that I believe my uncle killed the girls. Even worse is the possibility that all of his friends are involved, too. Maybe he's the one who's crazy."

Slipper moved to get more comfortable on the metal park bench. She thought they might be here a while yet. "You don't mean that. You're just upset with him. The more we get into this mess, the more suspects you have."

"I'm not saying you're wrong, and logically I can't believe he killed anyone. But his attitude towards my aunt bothers me. I have to ask myself, why am I so ready to make him the bad guy? I don't have an answer. I haven't ruled out Clare either. Deep down, I want it to be that photographer. This has become so personal."

Slipper saw all the strain on Sally's face, all the lines of doubt and worry.

"Life is never easy, Slipper. Sometimes it's downright impossible. I feel like I've been kicked in the stomach. It's hard to believe Clare could have killed her daughter, although I'm positive she knows who did. Sometimes, no matter how hard one tries to find the answer, there doesn't seem to be one." She let out a long breath. "Peter and I are going to do some serious work tonight, so hopefully we can work out a plan to help my aunt."

Sally stood up and started heading back towards the car.

"I can't go back to Peter's without seeing my aunt, so let's go and get it over with," Sally called back to her friend.

"Right," Slipper replied.

CHAPTER TWELVE
ANOTHER ATTACK

As Slipper pulled out into rush hour traffic, she found the familiar streets busy with other drivers like her, tired from a long day. But Slipper couldn't head back to the hotel just yet. Instead they drove back toward the courthouse.

At least it should be fairly quiet tonight, she thought.

Both girls were brought back from their wandering thoughts as Sally's cell phone, sitting on the dash, abruptly started to ring. The car swerved a bit, and Slipper chuckled.

Sally answered the call. "Sally here."

"Hi, it's just me," Peter said. "I guess you're on your way back to my place? Only I have to detour you. You asked me this morning about the doctor who's treating your aunt. He's your uncle's family physician, and it turns out he can have your aunt committed. They may try to have her declared insane. If they do, none of your efforts will hold water. Since you're quickly becoming a threat to their plans, I think we should move on this immediately."

"What do you mean by immediately?" Sally asked.

"Right now. I hope you don't mind, but I've just sent Dr. Sam Feldman, a good friend of mine, over to the courthouse lockup. He'll give your aunt an examination to check her mental stability.

CHAPTER TWELVE: ANOTHER ATTACK

He's very well known and a great guy. But it means you have to get over to the courthouse right away, in case he has any trouble getting in. Sam will be waiting for you there on the front steps."

Sally was slightly confused. "You mean right this minute?"

"Yes, I think we had better move fast. Things are getting rather complicated."

"Thanks, Peter. I honestly don't know what I would do without you."

"Hold on to that thought," he said. "I'll see you at home. Call me if you run into any trouble."

She dared not think of Peter or Mark and her feelings at this point. It was strange how alike they were, yet also very different.

As they drove, she explained to Slipper what Peter had shared with her and their urgent appointment with Dr. Feldman. In response, Slipper turned onto a side street that would get them to the courthouse more quickly.

"I think this is a good thing, Sally," Slipper said. "Wait and see what the doctor says. Peter seems to be right on the ball. You still have lots of time to make decisions."

Sally smiled at her. "Here I am, being tossed in every direction, and Peter comes up with a doctor. Every time I lose heart, an answer pops up. Hopefully, the doctor will agree that my aunt is fine, mentally speaking."

They soon pulled into the courthouse parking lot, which was almost empty.

"I think we've run into some good luck," Slipper said. "The building seems more or less closed, like the employees have gone home. Everyone probably left after we did." Slipper got out and locked the car. "Do we go inside or wait for the doctor out here?"

"Let's go to the front door. He should see us there." Sally led the way, her long legs covering the distance very quickly.

As they walked up onto the cement pad, Slipper observed that the building was very well-lit for the evening. She didn't like this at all. They were sitting ducks. She cast her eyes in every direction, looking for anything that spelled trouble.

After standing there for a good ten minutes, they saw the approach of a black Buick.

Sally felt a little worried about meeting this doctor Peter had sent. What if he found that her aunt was really ill? No, that wasn't even a possibility; she had to stop thinking that way. And he had better not belong to the ole boys club. She had to trust Peter on that.

The Buick pulled up right at the front door. Suddenly, Slipper stepped forward, drawing her gun.

"You're going to frighten the poor man to death," Sally remarked.

A short, podgy fellow emerged carrying an old-fashioned doctor's bag. He walked towards them briskly. Sally saw that he was well dressed and moved with ease.

He suddenly stopped when he saw the gun.

"You're going to rob me right in front of the courthouse?" he asked, staring at Slipper. "Peter didn't tell me to expect having a gun pointed at me."

"Who are you?" Sally spoke up, feeling a bit silly. Why was Slipper still holding a gun on the poor man?

"I'm Dr. Feldman, and I'm here to meet Lisa Cameron."

Sally moaned. "Oh Slipper, put the gun down. I'm sorry, Dr. Feldman, this is Slipper McKinnon and she's overprotecting me at the moment." Sally stepped out in front of her bodyguard, already able to tell that she could work with this man.

"Hi, Doc." Slipper put the gun down at her side. "I take my job as a bodyguard very seriously. If you don't mind, I'd like to see your driver's licence please. Take it out very slowly from your pocket."

CHAPTER TWELVE: ANOTHER ATTACK

Slipper watched his every move as she put his hand into his pocket and pulled out his wallet.

"Sally, please look… just to make sure. With threats hanging over our heads, I don't want to take any chances."

Sally studied the driver's license. "He is who he says he is."

"Good." Slipper put the gun back in her jeans. "I'll feel much better when we get inside. Sorry, Doctor, we've had a few close calls and someone is extremely interested in seeing Sally here very much dead. I presume you were alone in that car?"

"Yes, ma'am, I am alone. Care to check?"

"No, of course not," Sally interrupted. "Slipper is the most wonderful asset I've acquired since coming here. She's looking after me extremely well."

The doctor reached out his hand to Sally, then placed his other hand overtop hers. It was a very warm gesture, the sort that was usually reserved for ministers or very old men.

"Ms. Cameron, may I ask you a question? Two questions actually. First, do you believe your aunt's mind is normal, the same as most women her age?"

"Yes, I do, and maybe even better in some ways. She's always been very young at heart."

"Here's the second question: do you believe she killed those two girls?"

"I'm positive she didn't kill those girls. But then an awful feeling comes over me that leads me to think she may have. I have heard such incriminating stories. I barely know what's right and wrong anymore."

"Okay, let's go see your aunt."

They entered the front door and stopped at the counter. Sally folded her hands, trying to look calm. She didn't recognize the officer behind the desk, but there must be a good number of people who worked late hours.

"I'm Lisa Cameron's attorney," she began. "This is Sam Feldman and Slipper McKinnon. They're with me. I wish to see Mrs. Cameron please."

She didn't want to reveal that this man with them was a doctor, just in case.

"Sign here." The officer set a book on the counter. They grabbed pens and wrote their names on the lines provided. "Have you been here before?"

"Yes." That was all she was going to say. It was the truth—for her anyway.

"You may go ahead."

"Thank you." Sally smiled broadly and then turned, speaking to the doctor. "I think my aunt should be eating supper, or just finished. Does that matter?"

"No," he said as they stepped into a hallway. "I would like you to introduce me as a friend who's here to help you rather than her. Then, if she accepts that, leave me alone with her. You can stand just outside the door. If my word is going to be used in a courtroom, I must be sure of what I say. The interview will take about an hour. We'll talk about her meal, and possibly you, as a way of getting to know her and win her confidence."

"I understand," Sally said. "I'll do whatever you suggest."

There was no officer stationed right outside Lisa's door this time. When Sally pressed the button next to the door, it opened wide.

"I'll wait out here," Slipper said. She sat down in a chair.

They walked into the room, the doctor following Sally. But they stopped at the same time. The very quiet room was empty.

An uneasy feeling swept over Sally. "This is crazy. Where's my aunt?"

She looked to the doctor, totally confused, then back to the empty room. She couldn't believe her eyes.

CHAPTER TWELVE: ANOTHER ATTACK

For a moment, she wondered if her aunt had just gone to the bathroom. But the door to the bathroom was open, and the room beyond empty. Sally looked inside anyway, just to rule it out.

There had to be a simple explanation for this.

As she stood next to the yellow chair, the silliest thing happened: she started to cry. She turned away from the doctor; he didn't need to see her making such a fool of herself. Of all the ridiculous reactions to a crisis, tears were the worst. She needed to show common sense and quick thinking!

"Please, my dear, sit down." Dr. Feldman steered her into the yellow chair. "Sometimes tears are the very best medicine for stress. You've been through a lot since you arrived."

He took out a clean white cotton handkerchief and put it in her hands. It was a few minutes before she was under control again.

"You're right, I do feel better now," she said, drying her cheeks. "I should have been angry, not teary. Anyway, this may not be as bad as it looks. My aunt may have been moved to the jail to force my hand. My uncle and all his friends want me to go home."

"Take this one step at a time," said the doctor. "Let's go back to the front counter and demand to know where she's gone. You're her lawyer. They have to tell you where she is."

Sally was the first one out the door, her heart beating too fast. She could see that this was real trouble. She shook her head. How dare they try playing this game with her?

Slipper fell into step behind Sally, and the doctor did his best to keep up to the ladies with their long legs.

Peter had expected them to pull something on Sally, Slipper thought. *If they couldn't get rid of her, they had to succeed at getting her aunt away.*

Now there was going to be trouble. She hoped Peter was on top of this.

The officer at the desk looked up at their approach. "Yes?"

"Mrs. Cameron isn't in her room. Could you tell me where she has gone?" Sally tried to remain calm, suppressing a huge amount of anger.

"Really? I don't know, I've just come on shift. Excuse me a minute."

The officer walked over to another desk and leafed through several folders and papers on top of it. Behind her, another officer was working on a computer. They spoke together quietly. Sally couldn't hear what was being said, although she wished she could.

Soon the desk officer returned. "Ms. Cameron, I'm sorry no one called to inform you, but there was a problem with your client this afternoon."

"Just what kind of problem?" Sally asked, holding her breath. She refused to pay any attention to the tingling hairs on the back of her neck. This wasn't good.

"According to the report in front of me, she went absolutely crazy. She started to scream and several people tried to calm her down, but she refused their help. They finally had to call her doctor to sedate her. Her husband and the district attorney decided to take her to Mount Merry Meadow, where she can be properly looked after."

Be calm, she told herself. *Don't start screaming, or they'll take you there, too.*

"I see," Sally said. "And what time of day was this?"

"Just after lunch, around one o'clock. She also threw her tray of food at the officer who brought it in to her. I'm sorry. Is there anything else I can do for you?"

"No, thank you very much."

Sally turned away from the officer, feeling so angry that she could chew nails and spit rust. Her aunt was just as sane as she herself was! The murder had been a setup from day one.

CHAPTER TWELVE: ANOTHER ATTACK

"There has to be something we can do," Sally said aloud when they got outside. "I simply can't sit back and do nothing."

"I'm sorry to say this, but I'm probably too late to help her now," Dr. Feldman said. "They'll drug her for safety's sake, and I won't be able to give her a proper evaluation, even if I could get in to see her. We need to talk to Peter. He's clever and has a lot of pull in this city."

Slipper was looking in all directions. "Look, you two, I don't like Sally standing out here on the steps. Can we go somewhere, anywhere, private?"

"Come sit in my car for a few minutes," the doctor suggest. "It's closer than yours."

Slipper nodded in agreement as Sally slowly followed the man, feeling she had been defeated. Uncle Hill had won, and her aunt had lost.

"I'll stand out here," Slipper said as Sally opened the door to the passenger seat. "I'd like to keep watch."

"You're sure? I want you to know what's going on."

"I'm okay. Just leave the window down. I can hear just fine."

The next few minutes happened so fast that Sally wasn't even sure what hit her. She was talking to Dr. Feldman, leaning forward so Slipper could hear what she was saying, when she heard a crash; the front window burst into a great spider web.

The doctor grabbed for Sally, throwing her to the floor. He somehow landed in a heap on top of her. The glass hung suspended in the frame, its tiny threads looking like spun boiled sugar.

Slipper didn't have time to think. She hit the road beside the car. Someone was shooting at them, but from where?

"Don't move," Dr. Feldman said to Sally. Every bone hurt in his twisted body.

"Are you all right, Sally, Doctor?" Slipper yelled. "Sally, answer me!"

117

The doctor tried to get up, but he could barely move. "Yes, we're all right, other than that Sally is being squeezed to death."

"I'm calling the cops. I'm sure the gunfire came from your side of the car. Keep down!"

Slipper quickly took out her phone and dialled 911, and the operator dispatched help right away.

"How are you?" Sally called to Slipper.

"I'm fine. I should go after the shooter, but I'm not going to. I don't trust him not to double back, and I don't know that he's gone, either. Just stay down for a few minutes more."

Dr. Feldman shifted over to one side, trying to keep his head down. "Sorry, my dear," he said to Sally. "I admit I'm a bit overweight."

Sally had no idea if she was or wasn't all right. She had been shoved partly to the floor and wasn't sure what to do now.

"Stay put," Slipper called again. "Keep your heads down until the police arrive."

Within minutes, cops appeared all over the place, with more coming. Slipper was going crazy trying to explain what had happened. It was lucky for her that she knew several of the cops.

According to one officer, whoever had shot at them hadn't used a powerful enough gun to actually penetrate the windshield. That would suggest an amateur, assuming of course that the shooter had intended to kill them.

An hour later, the police found a few empty shell casings from a rifle.

Slipper gave the cops a report as to what happened, talked to the inspector in charge, and then they were free to go. Slipper was pleased, in a way. The incident had succeeded in alerting the police to the fact that what Sally was saying should be taken seriously.

CHAPTER TWELVE: ANOTHER ATTACK

"I'm sorry, I probably crushed you," the doctor said to Sally again as they sat on the pavement. "I didn't think. When I heard the glass crack, I just pushed you down."

"And probably saved my life," Sally pointed out. "That seems to be the name of the game—see how close you can get to killing Sally. I know, it isn't a joke."

Slipper sat down in the back seat. "Whoever our shooter was, they don't know much about guns. Or maybe it was just another scare tactic to try and get rid of you. If your uncle is behind this, I can't see him wanting to kill you. Scaring you makes more sense. But why now, when they've more or less won? Maybe they're still trying to gain more time. We've lost a couple of hours." She paused, still thinking through the events of the last few hours. "Whoever did the shooting is probably far away by now, you can bet on that."

"I think you ladies have had enough for tonight," said the doctor. "You should go home. Maybe tomorrow we can talk again."

"Well, the longer my aunt is in that asylum, the harder it will be to prove she's in her right mind." Sally took a deep breath. "And the drugs will make it impossible after a while. There has to be a way to get her out of their hands. At least this proves how right I've been all along. That makes me feel a lot better."

Sally picked up her cell phone and pushed a few buttons.

"Could I please speak to Peter Matthews, if he's still there?" Sally said to the person who answered. "This is Sally Cameron. He's waiting for my call."

"Sure, just hold on a second."

A few moments passed. "Peter here. Did the doctor get to see your aunt?"

"Peter, they've already taken her to that mental institution I was telling you about earlier. It seems they took her away this afternoon. I'm an idiot. I should have seen it coming."

"Is Sam there with you now?"

"Yes, he is."

"Put him on the line for a minute."

"Peter wants to talk to you." Sally handed the phone to the doctor, almost afraid of what the two men were going to talk about.

"Peter, it's Sam here. What Sally says is correct."

"Listen carefully. This is exactly what we were afraid of." Peter proceeded to give him very detailed instructions. "Sam, I don't want Sally to know what we're up to. I don't want to jeopardize her position or get her upset. Now, let me talk to Slipper."

Next, Slipper took the phone.

Don't tell him about the shooting, Sally mouthed to her.

As Slipper and Peter spoke, Sally became bothered by the fact that she could tell they were talking about something Peter didn't want her to know about.

"Look, Slipper," Sally said once her friend ended the call. "I can tell something is going on. Surely I can help."

Slipper nodded. "I agree you can help, but we must not do anything you could later be blamed for, as your aunt's lawyer."

"Yes, all right."

Slipper had to smile. Sally accepted that a little too easily.

"Sam," Slipper said, turning to the doctor, "Peter wants us to visit that institution to see Mrs. Cameron. They won't let Peter in, so it has to be us. He'll meet up with us after we finish."

For their trip to Mount Merry Meadow, they decided to take Sally's car. In the meantime, Dr. Feldman called for a tow truck to take his Buick away.

"Sam, I'm sorry about your car," Sally said, staring at the broken glass. "I'll pay for your windshield and any other damage. After all, it was my fault. It's the least I can do."

CHAPTER TWELVE: ANOTHER ATTACK

"Let's not worry about it. I have insurance. The important thing is that we're all safe and well."

They got into Sally's car, Slipper behind the wheel and the doctor in the passenger's seat. Slipper wanted Sally safely in the back seat, out of sight in case the shooter was still around.

CHAPTER THIRTEEN
WHAT NOW?

Slipper drove to Mount Merry Meadow, following Dr. Feldman's directions, as he had visited several times in the past to see patients. Twenty minutes later, they drove down a laneway right up to huge iron gates that were securely fastened. A great sign hung in front reading No Admittance. Slipper stopped the car. There was no way to get in.

"There's a speaker and a camera," Dr. Feldman pointed out. "I suggest we go right up to it and state our business. I've never had a problem, although I've never been here so late."

Despite speaking with the staff inside, however, nobody would let them in until visiting hours tomorrow—and even then, they'd only allow Sally inside, as Lisa's lawyer.

After giving up, Sally's phone went off. It was Peter, wanting to meet them right away at a nearby coffee shop. She agreed, and within a few minutes they were back on the main road, this time heading south.

The coffee shop was almost empty at this time of night. Slipper parked right beside Peter's old beat-up car, seeing his anxious face through the window the minute they parked. She was sure they hadn't been followed.

CHAPTER THIRTEEN: WHAT NOW?

"People, please don't tell Peter about the shooting," Sally said. "He has enough on his mind without worrying about me. I'm fine. All that matters to me right now is getting Dr. Feldman in to see my aunt."

Sally got out of the car and embraced Peter in the parking lot.

"Are you all right?" Peter grabbed Sally and hugged her, then pulled back, reluctant to let her go, his eyes hungrily ingesting everything about her. "You look great."

"Yes, we're all fine. But I do need some help."

He knew that he had to keep her fighting for what she believed in. She was on the right track. And no matter if Judge Cameron was innocent of the girls' death, Peter knew he would face charges before this was over.

"Look, we have some serious talking to do," Peter said. "Could we talk in your car, Sally? No one will bother us there. I worry that the coffee shop is too open."

"Good idea," Dr. Feldman agreed.

Slipper, feeling like she had little to add, decided to stand watch from a short distance away.

"I have a bit to tell you," Peter began once he was settled beside Dr. Feldman in the back seat of the car. "Although I can't yet tell you everything that's happening right now."

"I don't understand." Sally made eye contact with Peter. She wanted everyone to be on the same page.

"One advantage to being a reporter is that we sometimes learn more about what's going on than the police. We have our sources. But first, I need you to fill me in about everything that happened earlier in the courthouse."

Sally began with their visit to see her aunt, continuing right until the present moment. But she left out the shooting.

"We got word this afternoon from a guy I know who's watching the courthouse," Peter said. "He says that an ambulance pulled up to the back entrance around eleven-thirty. It stayed for just a few minutes. He took some pictures, but they show very little—just someone on a stretcher. We can't be sure it was your aunt, but Judge Cameron was there. We have pictures of him coming and going. They should be useable in court. We also have two shots of the district attorney at the back door. No matter what happened, she had no business being there. Then Judith and the judge followed the ambulance in a car to Mount Merry Meadow. Judith could claim she was there because your aunt was under arrest, but that's a stretch." He looked from Sally to the doctor. "My friends and I are going to put a plan into operation soon for the doctor to see your aunt. Just leave it to me. The police are asking questions, and that's good. We just have to be patient a little while longer."

He reached over and put his hand behind Sally's head, then pulled her forward and gave her a kiss, not caring that the doctor was right there.

"Sally, please don't do anything without me knowing it. I don't want anything to happen to you. Now, I have to go and Sam's coming with me. Ready, Sam?"

"Sure, whatever you say," Dr. Feldman said. It seemed clear to him that Peter was in love with Sally, and who could blame him?

The doctor got into Peter's car. Sally watched as they drove away.

"Let's go home," Sally called to the approaching Slipper. "Funny how easy it is to call Peter's place my home, even though I don't live there."

While driving down the highway, Slipper was careful to keep well within the speed limit. Before long, they turned off onto the country road that led to Peter's property.

Sally was glad to see the house she was now calling home; she dared not think of it any other way. She needed to feel secure. They walked up to the front door, turned the handle, and walked inside.

"I guess you'll sleep in the same room you did before," Sally said. "Almira is probably in bed."

"Yeah right! Believe me, count to ten and Almira will be standing there, wide awake." Slipper smiled. "There's something in the Aboriginal spirit. I don't think she sleeps. If she does, it's with one eye open."

Just a few seconds later, they heard a swishing sound. Almira's pleasant face shone out at them from hallway.

"The boss said you would be late," Almira said in her housecoat. "He's going to be a long time, too, and says we should put your friend in the pretty blue room. She stayed there before."

Sally nodded. "Yes, I know, Almira. We're going to bed. See you tomorrow morning."

"Do you want hot chocolate or tea?" the housekeeper asked.

"No thanks, Almira." Sally said. "We're too tired."

Slipper turned back to her friend. "Sally, I'll see you in the morning. Please sleep with your windows locked tonight. I'm going to take a look outside before I go to bed. I'll knock on your door to let you know I'm inside later and that everything's fine."

Almira looked at her, shocked. "You going for a walk past midnight? Outside in the pitch black? There may be wild animals out there!"

"I just want to make sure there are no bad guys lurking around," Slipper explained. "The animals I can handle."

"No bad guys around here." Almira laughed and laughed. "Just in the city. We're safe here."

"Still… I'd like to see for myself."

"You wait."

With that, Almira trotted down the hall, slippers flopping at her heels. Her bright red housecoat flowed behind her as she disappeared from sight.

"Well, what do you make of that?" Slipper asked. "I always knew she was a queer duck."

"I have no idea. Maybe she's going with you." Sally chuckled. "As no one knows I'm here, I don't think you have anything to worry about."

"We're *presuming* no one knows you're here. I just want to be sure. Remember, Peter hired me to keep you safe. Go to bed. A walk won't hurt me anyhow."

Slipper only got halfway down the hall before she was met by an anxious Almira and a short man, also of Aboriginal persuasion. He was wearing a pair of jeans and plaid shirt. He carried a shotgun and had a dog sitting by his side. The dog didn't issue a snarl or a bark, but it looked at her very alert, its nose sniffing in Slipper's direction.

"Did you hear something unusual?" the man asked in a deep voice.

Slipper had never seen him before. "No, not exactly. Who are you?"

"I'm Red Eagle, like the sun shining on birds in the sky. I'm Mr. Peter's protector."

"Funny man," Almira said. "He's my husband, Fred, protector of himself."

"The boss called me, so I'll go looking for whatever upset you." Fred suddenly seemed to stand a little taller. He pointed at the dog. "This here is Prince Albert. He's the best watchdog and a very good animal."

Slipper certainly wasn't going to disagree with that. "All right, let's go together."

She started ahead, just like Fred and the dog weren't there. She felt somewhat better having the company, but she wasn't sure about the shotgun.

Fred walked beside her, the dog keeping within a few feet of them.

CHAPTER THIRTEEN: WHAT NOW?

As they circled the house, Slipper watched all around her. She was thankful for the bright moon tonight. The house's windows and doors were all well secured.

They searched for twenty minutes, finding no sign of intruders. She figured their conversation would have scared anyone off if they had been about.

Later, Slipper knocked on Sally's door, then carried on into her own room. She had a quick shower and fell asleep in minutes, thinking that with the big chief on the grounds they were quite safe.

* * *

Sally lay awake that night, unable to sleep. She reluctantly sat up, picked up her purse, and took out her phone. She knew what Peter had said, but she felt the need to call her father. She dialled his number and waited for him to answer. Then, remembering the time difference, she decided he must be in bed.

"Hello, Cameron residence."

"Dad, I forgot the time difference. Did I wake you?"

"No, I was sitting here waiting for your call," he said. "You were supposed to come home on the next flight out of Regina. You know, Hilliard called me a little while ago, very disturbed. He seems to think he's fighting you as well as the police for your aunt's safety. He had to remove her from the jail for her own safety. He says he can't reach you now and doesn't know where you're staying." He sounded so upset. "Sally, this isn't like you and I'm worried. You've gotten much too close to this thing and it's blocking your good judgment. You remember the ridiculous mistakes your sister made? They almost ruined our lives. Don't make the same mistakes."

"Dad, I think Uncle Hill is the one who's sick," Sally insisted. "Aunt Lisa told me she wants to divorce him, and right now I don't blame her. I know he's my uncle and your brother, but when something's wrong, it's wrong. There is no grey area here."

"Sally, you just don't understand what's at stake. Whose life do you think is more important? Sometimes one has to be sacrificed to make way for many. Grow up, Sally!"

"Maybe that's the problem. I *have* grown up."

Sally was so angry. There were no words to express her misery.

"Sally, I think we've talked enough. Call again when you've had some time to think about what I've said. You'll see how wrong you are. And I think you should talk to Mark, too. I know he's worried about you. What's your number over there?"

"Forget it, Dad. I no longer trust you."

Sally sat on the edge of the bed, then decided to end the call without even saying good night. Maybe she was acting like a spoiled child.

No, I'm an adult, she reminded herself. *Even more important, I'm a professional lawyer. How could he do this to me?*

Sally climbed back into bed and said her prayers.

CHAPTER FOURTEEN
NEW LODGINGS

Morning light shone through the window, sunbeams dancing all over the walls. Sally opened her eyes and felt like she had only just gone to sleep.

She pushed the covers back and sat up, quickly. Standing, she put her body through several exercises that were part of her everyday routine. They helped to get her blood flowing and clear her mind.

After yesterday, she needed the Lord—and there was only one way to get to him when it was this important. She fell to her knees beside the bed and began to pray. She shed a few tears, knowing that God would look after her aunt, who was a good Christian woman.

Sally made her way towards the kitchen, wondering what time Peter had come in. She also wondered what she would do if the staff at Mount Merry Meadow refused to let her see her aunt. If they ignored that piece of paper with her aunt's signature, Sally would have no rights.

In the kitchen, Almira was happily baking and kneading dough.

"Ah, she's awake," Slipper said.

"Good morning." A large yawn escaped Sally's mouth. "Almira, thank you very much for washing my jeans. I appreciate it. Is Peter still sleeping?"

"No, ma'am," Almira said. "Not seen Peter since yesterday. He's been out a long time, but not to worry."

"Isn't that nice of Almira to worry about Peter?" Slipper said in a droll voice.

Sally was surprised. "He hasn't come back?"

Almira kept working the dough. "No, ma'am, he's still away."

"Do you know where he's gone?"

"No, ma'am."

Almira brought her a glass of orange juice in her floury hands, followed by a coffee. Next came hot cereal, summer or not. Then a corn muffin and more coffee.

Slipper grinned. "Eat up, chum. At least she's an amazing cook. She's fattening you up for Peter."

Sally turned away and switched on the television to hear the morning news.

"—has been missing since sometime early this morning," the news anchor said. "Here is the woman's description: she's five-foot-four, weighs about one hundred and twenty pounds, and is seventy years old. She's not dangerous. Please call the police if anyone has any information. The police are also trying to locate her niece, Ms. Salesian 'Sally' Cameron, a visitor to our city…"

Slipper looked to Sally in surprise, questions written all over her face as the anchor went on. Sally changed the channel and heard similar announcements on other news reports.

"Slipper, do you realize what they're saying? My aunt is missing! That must mean she's not at Mount Merry Meadow after all, and they think I have her. What in the world could they have done with her? And they're trying to blame me!"

"It sure sounds that way," Slipper said.

"I have to talk to Peter."

Slipper put up a hand. "Wait a minute. They might have moved her to another institution in case you brought reinforcements today. You kind of threatened them, remember? I'm sure wherever Peter is, he's aware of the news broadcasts just like you are. He's probably already looking into it."

As she said this, Slipper realized that she had a good idea of what had happened to Lisa. But if Sally didn't catch on, she'd better not say anything for the time being.

"Almira, do you know where the phone book is?" Sally asked.

"Sure, ma'am. In that drawer under the phone."

"Thank you. Oh, and has a doctor named Sam Feldman ever been here that you know of?"

"Sure, ma'am, he's a good friend of the boss. A real nice man."

"It's his phone number I need."

"Sure, ma'am. It's in the funny flip thing"—she used her arm to demonstrate—"on the boss's desk."

"Great, thanks a lot."

Sally trotted off to the library where she knew Peter had a desk, Slipper following right behind her. She headed straight for the rolodex in question, and a minute later she was dialling the numbers on Peter's phone. Slipper stood back near the door, leaning against the frame.

"Good morning, Dr. Feldman's office."

It was a receptionist.

"I'm sorry to bother you, but my name is Sally and I need to talk with Sam. It's very important." She was hoping that using first names might get her faster service.

"I'm sorry, Sally who?"

"Look, please just tell him that I'm on the line. It's very personal and important."

"Personal... Madam, most of the doctor's calls are personal. Can I get him to call you back?"

Sally hesitated for a moment, then smiled. "Would you tell him it's one of the tall blondes he was with last night? After our evening, I know he'll talk to me."

There was silence on the line. Sally could almost hear the receptionist's breathing and startled facial expression.

"Are you sure you have the right person? Dr. Sam Feldman?"

"Oh yes, believe me, I have the right Sam. We were very close last night."

That poor man will never live this call down, Slipper thought from the doorway.

The receptionist didn't bite. "I still didn't get your last name."

This was getting her nowhere. "Please, this is very important. If you would just speak to him—"

"Believe me, whoever you are, I would like to do just that. But he left a message on my machine cancelling all his appointments for the next two days. That's all I know. If you know something, I would appreciate you telling me. I'm very worried about him."

"Ah, okay. That's fine. I know where he is then. You don't have to worry. Thanks so much." She ended the conversation with the press of one little button. Sally had to smile, spotting Slipper's grin. "I hope I didn't suddenly create a problem, if there was something between Sam and his secretary."

"On the other hand, it may make life more interesting for them," Slipper said. "The problem now is that your aunt is an escaped prisoner, and a suspected murderer. I can't think of anything more threatening to you than that." She stepped further into the room. "I'm sure the minute the institution noticed your aunt missing, they called your uncle, who in turned called the police, and he would have named you immediately. That is, if he wasn't himself responsible for taking her."

CHAPTER FOURTEEN: NEW LODGINGS

Sally sighed. "I need another cup of coffee."

They were about to leave the library when the telephone rang again—just once. Almira must have answered it somewhere else in the house. Both women looked to the door, waiting for Almira to come through to explain that Peter had called.

"Sally," Almira called. "Sally!"

It was just a few minutes before Almira entered, telephone in hand.

"I couldn't find you!" she added. "It's for you, ma'am. It's the boss."

Sally put the phone to her ear. "Peter?"

"Hi. Have you had the television on?"

"Yes."

"I'll be by in a few minutes with a rental car for you and Slipper to use," Peter said. "That way, we won't be so easily connected. I've also found another place for you and Slipper to stay temporarily. So be ready to go, with your bags packed. Just take your clothes, none of the work on your aunt's case. I'll answer your questions when I see you." He cleared his throat. "By the way, your aunt is fine."

She didn't have time to say thanks or anything. He just disconnected the line.

"Let's go then," Slipper said after Sally repeated everything. "Get your things, fast."

The excitement was back in Slipper's voice, and she felt her adrenaline pump.

A few minutes later, she and Sally were waiting at the back of the house, pacing back and forth, their minds running in a dozen different directions.

Peter picked them up in the rental car, one with dark-tinted windows, about twenty minutes later. They fastened their seatbelts as Peter took off again.

"We're on our way to a safe place," Peter explained. "Slipper, keep your eyes on Sally more carefully than ever. And Sally, you need to go to the cops, now that they're looking for you. They can't hold you on anything, neither of you, but you need to come forward right away. If anyone asks who referred Slipper to you, just say it was a good friend. That's all they need to know. I just want you to know that I'm not letting you down, but I'm too involved to be close to you right now. You have my cell phone number if you need me. If for some reason you can't reach me, call me at work, but be mindful what you say to my secretary. I'm going to be busy for the next few days, helping your aunt. That's all I'm going to tell you."

"Peter, do you know where my aunt is?"

"That's one of the questions you can't ask. It's like I don't know you and you don't know me. We've never met—that is, unless they tie us together from that one dinner we went to together. Well, I'll worry about that if it happens. There are powerful men involved in this and we can't trust them. Just think what must be going through their minds, not knowing where your aunt disappeared to." Peter turned onto another road and kept driving. "I'm providing you with a place to stay at a bed-and-breakfast. Sally, as far as anyone is concerned, you're just the innocent niece worrying about what happened to your aunt and demanding that the police do something to find her. If you're up to it, accuse your uncle of kidnapping her. That's what the other side is doing—blaming you. So turn the tables."

Peter slowed down and pulled in front of a beautiful house with a bed-and-breakfast sign on the front lawn.

"Ah, here we are," he said. "Come on in. I'll explain as we go."

They got out of the car and began walking up a path around the house to the back door.

"By the way, I also heard about the shooting," Peter added. "Sally, you stay glued to Slipper. This is serious, and that shooter means business. With your aunt missing, that's probably eased the danger for the time being. But if they think you have her, they'll follow you. So be careful."

Peter didn't hesitate at the door; he just opened it and motioned them inside. She followed, somewhat hesitantly, right at his heels.

As Peter proceeded into the kitchen, Sally decided that he knew exactly where he was going.

"Hi sweetheart, how are you doing?" Peter said to the young woman sitting at the kitchen table drinking a can of pop. They hugged and Peter kissed her cheek. "Once again, you're an answer to my prayers."

"Yeah right," the woman said. "Is this the young lady you were talking about?"

"Yes, isn't she beautiful? Not to say her friend isn't, too, of course."

The woman stood up, recognizing Slipper. "Hi, Slipper. We should be familiar with this dangerous lifestyle, yet he still gets us, right?"

Sally noted that the woman was a few years younger than herself, attractive, and average height and weight. She even had Peter's colouring and knew Slipper.

"This is my sister, Martha," Peter said. "She owns and runs this establishment. She usually has a full house, so we're lucky she has room for you right now."

"Peter likes to keep things in the family," Slipper said.

Peter nodded. "Sit down, relax a minute, and Martha will show you to your rooms. Then I'm off. I've already explained the story to Martha, that we've never met and that you came here right from the airport. I haven't been here to visit for a while either. Sally, you can completely trust Martha. She's a really good person." He ran a hand through his hair. "Remember, Sally, after you go to the cops, you'll be followed from that moment on. If Slipper has to take you to my place, she'll have to make sure to lose your tail."

Peter was moving so fast that Sally couldn't follow half of what was happening.

"Sally and Slipper will be back later, Martha," Peter said to his sister. "If for some reason they don't show up by midnight, call me right away. I don't want you all getting to be friends either. Don't tell Martha anything. That way she doesn't need to get involved."

"You know, it would be nice if you didn't talk like I wasn't even here," Martha said.

"You're here and we're playing a dangerous game. Sally's life has already been threatened twice. Be careful. I owe you one for this."

He stopped and looked at Sally, then walked up to her. He picked her up off the chair where she'd sat down, pulled her tightly to him, and kissed her. She stood there in a daze, watching the back of him walk away.

"Sam Feldman, eat your heart out," Peter said as he left the house.

Slipper laughed and Martha nearly passed out from shock. Sally felt numb, stunned. No one had ever kissed her like that, not even Mark.

"Never mind, you'll get used to this, Martha," Slipper said. "This is going to be interesting! But I owe you an apology, and I'm not sure where to start. After all, Peter asked me not to tell you anything. Thank you for having me here, though. I will pay you when I leave, or give you a cheque now if you like."

"Oh, don't worry about that. Peter's already paid for two weeks." Martha stood up. "Now, if you'll follow me, I'll take you to your rooms."

Not long after, she handed Sally a key and led her into an old-fashioned room full of beautiful antiques. The central attraction was an amazing quilted blanket, covered in shades of blue, and obviously homemade.

"This quilt is gorgeous," Sally remarked.

"My mother made it. I have one in different shades for each of my rooms. Needless to say, this is the blue room."

Sally smiled at Martha, thinking that she liked Peter's sister as much as she liked Peter himself.

"Slipper, you're right next door," Martha said.

As she showed Slipper in, she showed her that this room and Sally's were adjoining and could be opened from either side with a key.

"Thanks so much," Slipper said. "Again, you have no idea how much I appreciate this."

An hour later, Slipper and Sally made their way out the back door, approaching the rental car. Sally wasn't looking forward to going to the police station, but they had to get it over with.

* * *

In the police station parking lot, Sally got out of the sleek car, adjusting her skirt, which had managed to lift a little too high. Slipper locked the vehicle behind them.

"Let's get this show on the road," Sally said.

They both strode with purpose toward the building. Sally stopped at the front door, not sure what to expect when she walked in. She had been dreading this moment.

"This won't be so bad," Slipper said. "Relax and just remember that you don't know Peter. On everything else, stick to the truth and it'll all be fine. You have every right to be upset."

They walked inside, Sally closing the door behind them and quickly surveying the surroundings.

No one had so far even noticed them. Either that, or the staff was deliberately ignoring them. Slipper hadn't seen anyone she knew either. Then again, she had left the force almost five years ago.

Gosh no, she thought. *It's closer to six. Where did the time go?*

"Excuse me," Sally said to the uniformed officer behind the counter. "I heard on the morning news that you're looking for Salesian Cameron. Well, that's me, and I'm quite upset. I'd like to see whoever's in charge of the Lisa Cameron case."

"Yes, ma'am," the male officer said. "You are Sally Cameron, the old lady's attorney?"

"No, sir. I'm Lisa Cameron's attorney, not some old lady." She saw by the expression on his face that she had his attention.

"I'm sorry, ma'am. Do you have any identification with you?"

Sally took out her driver's licence and showed it to the officer.

"I'm sorry, ma'am, for the delay. I will get you someone right away."

Slipper chose that moment to stick her head around Sally, moving right up to the counter.

"Ma'am, are you two together?"

"Yes, we are," Slipper said. "Would Inspector Malvern or Chief Markell be in, by any chance?" She looked to Sally to explain. "I worked for William Malvern a few years ago." Then, turning back to the desk officer, she added, "I retired about six years ago when I got married. I work for the department part-time now."

"Chief Markell is very busy at the moment." He leaned in toward Slipper. "You'd better expect to wait a while." Next, he addressed Sally. "If you'll please sit down, I'll let the chief's secretary know you're here."

"Okay, thank you."

Sally noticed plenty of chairs along the wall. She walked towards them and sat down. Slipper sat beside her, not sure what

CHAPTER FOURTEEN: NEW LODGINGS

to say. The cop at the desk looked at her unhappily, but she just grinned back.

"He's just a staff sergeant," Slipper said softly. "Not that they're unimportant."

Slipper was wondering why she hadn't seen one person she knew yet. She thought about getting up and asking who was on duty, running several names over in her mind. She did a lot of undercover work for Vice, on the second floor. Someone had to be here.

"Excuse me, Ms. Cameron," the desk sergeant called over. "The chief will see you now, if you'll just follow me."

"Thank you, I would appreciate that." She thought it was about time; her patience was wearing thin.

She followed the officer along a hall until they came to a door with a plaque inscribed with the chief's name. Slipper had stayed right by her side the whole way.

The officer knocked on the door, then entered.

"The chief is expecting us," he said to the secretary, then turned to the ladies. "Please, come this way." He knocked on a door and entered right away. He stood at attention. "Chief, this is Ms. Cameron and Ms. McKinnon.

"Thank you, Staff Sergeant." Markell got to his feet and immediately shook hands with the women. "I'm so sorry for all the trouble you've been through since coming to Regina. We're normally such a lovely, friendly city." He flagged down the staff sergeant before he could leave. "Excuse me one minute. When you get back to the desk, please see that the all-points bulletin is lifted on Ms. Cameron and make sure everyone is aware of this."

The women sat, and suddenly Markell's face brightened, as though seeing Slipper for the first time.

"Slipper, it's good to see you." He smiled at them. "Please ladies, sit down."

They both sat in chairs across from the chief's desk.

"I have to ask one question before we get down to business. Did you kidnap your aunt from Mount Merry Meadow?" Markell asked. "Then again, how could one lone woman, even if you had Slipper's help, possibly steal an old lady from that iron-fenced place?"

"I had nothing to do with it," Sally said.

Markell nodded. "Okay. I never for one minute believed your aunt killed anyone, let alone two prostitutes. I called in one of our best detectives, Chief Inspector North Miller, and put him on the case yesterday. I'm sure he can straighten out the whole mess."

"I'm thankful someone else agrees with me," Sally said, feeling relieved.

The chief drummed his fingers on the desk, his lack of patience causing his nerves to fray slightly. As chief, Markell was fully aware of what was going on and he wasn't happy about it. Sally Cameron was probably a top-notch lawyer, by her look. And he couldn't blame her for being concerned about her aunt.

Where are you, North? he asked himself. *Pick up that phone and call me.*

"There are never enough men in the department to cover all the crime we have here," Markell mused. "But that's another story. The government could do all of us a good service by getting us some more men."

Sally felt sorry for the man. Obviously she had surprised him by showing up here. Now he was doing his best to make things right. Then again, shouldn't he what everything that was going on, with all those details being printed in the papers? Maybe he was just passing the buck, so to speak.

"I do wish North would get here," Markell said. "Just give us a couple of minutes. He can't be far."

CHAPTER FIFTEEN
WHERE AM I?

Blossom sat in a chair by the open window, a warm breeze flowing about the room this morning. Her grey hair reflected a sheen from the morning sun coming through the pane of glass between the soft yellow curtains.

She sat in a comfortable stuffed chair, her back straight, with no stoop for a lady eighty-five years young. She was a woman familiar with hard work and struggle and had raised a family on a reservation where their domain had been a small village.

Blossom looked over at the sleeping lady in bed, knowing that after she'd arrived last night, she had been drugged with warm milk to make her sleep. She was still in a deep slumber.

* * *

Lisa opened her eyes and for a minute she didn't think things looked right. She seemed to be quite alone in a strange bed.

I should be used to that by now, she thought groggily.

She lay very still, frightened and not knowing where she was. She also felt as though she was being watched. She decided to play dead, so to speak, like a dog.

Her whole body ached from tension. She could so easily scream, only that would make her jailers angry. In the stillness, she turned her head this way and that, suddenly remembering she wasn't in lockup anymore. They had taken her to that other awful place.

She also remembered someone had taken her from her room last night, and she hadn't known where they were going. A woman had said that Sally was waiting for her at the place where they were taking her; she just had to cooperate and be quiet.

Lisa remembered thinking that nothing could be as bad as where she was, so she gave in. They'd taken her to a house and given her a warm glass of milk. She'd drank it and then passed out.

Where was she?

She rubbed her eyes with the back of her hand and sat up in the bed, surprised to see an older lady sitting in a chair beside the window.

"Good morning," the woman said, smiling. "Well, you decided to wake up, did you? It's a beautiful day today. Don't be alarmed or frightened, Mrs. Cameron, you're quite safe here. Take your time. If you'll get up and follow me, I'll take you to a bathroom where you can shower and put on these clothes." She held up some things in her arms.

Lisa looked at her, not sure if she dared do what she said. Everything was so confusing.

"Don't be afraid. You are among friends. So much has happened to you over the past few days that you must be very confused, even frightened. However, you're safe here."

Lisa nearly panicked. Nothing looked familiar. The woman seemed to be kind and friendly, and the room looked very nice, but appearances could be deceiving.

"Where exactly am I?" Lisa asked.

"A safe place, and that is really all I can say for now. If you'll follow me, I'll show you where the bathroom is and you can ready yourself for the day."

CHAPTER FIFTEEN: WHERE AM I?

"Thank you. That will be fine." Lisa did just that, then followed her along a long hallway past several closed doors.

Blossom put down the clothes and a small cosmetics bag on a chair. "I will be back in twenty minutes or so. Please don't try to leave without me, or I'll have to lock you in the room and I don't want to do that."

"This appears to be a house," Lisa said, trying to make sense of her situation. "Is this a smaller mental institution?"

"That's the first time I've ever heard someone refer to a house that way." She laughed. "Although to be honest, my daughter might feel that way sometimes. No, ma'am, it's just a house and you need to stay here for a while till your niece straightens out a few things. Please, go have a shower. Then we can have breakfast."

Lisa decided on a quick shower that lasted five minutes. She was out and dressed in no time, in clothes that weren't hers, although they were clean. Maybe that was all that mattered. She had no idea where they had come from. Still, they were simple, plain, and comfortable.

Lisa looked up as the woman appeared again as she finished dressing. "Mrs. Cameron, your breakfast is ready."

Once again, Lisa followed her along a hallway with several closed doors. She then entered a small kitchen.

"Please sit down, ma'am," said a younger woman carrying a glass of ice-cold orange juice.

Lisa was served the juice, cereal, toast, two fried eggs, and three strips of bacon. The food was excellent, and she was very hungry.

After she had eaten, she looked around only to find that the older woman had left. The younger woman, though, sat down at the other side of the table with a cup of coffee.

"Thank you," said Lisa. "That was delicious."

"You're welcome. Do you mind if I take a few minutes to drink some coffee here before cleaning up? Some mornings require more caffeine than others." She filled her cup with more coffee. "Coffee is the magic ingredient to an early morning start."

"That would be fine. Is this your house? I have to say, I'm so terribly confused."

"It is, in a way. Mine and the banks, if you know what I mean."

The attractive young woman's complexion told Lisa that she was Aboriginal.

"Do you know why I'm here?" Lisa asked.

"Not really, but you don't have to be afraid. My brother said you are to stay here for a while. I'm sure everything will be all right."

"I see. Are you my kidnappers, the same ones who took those dreadful pictures of my husband?"

"No! Please, we mean you no harm. We're not kidnappers and we didn't take any pictures. I was told they were bringing you here to keep you safe. Your niece felt you were in some kind of danger. Anyway, all I know is what I was told. Please don't ask me any more questions or you'll get me in trouble." The woman stood up, hoping Lisa would follow. This poor old lady was really mixed up. "Will you follow me back to the sitting room?"

Lisa followed her back to a sitting room and sat in an armchair.

"Now, Mrs. Cameron, I'd like you to stay in this nice room until lunchtime. Here's a glass of water with ice in case you get thirsty." She sat the glass on a small table beside the large stuffed chair. "There's also a plate of homemade cookies and two good books, if you care to read, or several magazines. I'll be along from time to time to see if there's anything you want or need. Please don't leave the room, or I'll have to lock you in the bedroom. Sorry, I'm just following orders."

The young woman turned and walked out of the room.

Lisa watched her leave. By all accounts, this place certainly appeared to be an ordinary house. The question was, whose?

CHAPTER FIFTEEN: WHERE AM I?

She had no idea where she was, but she didn't sense any danger at all. She smiled to herself. She wouldn't necessarily know danger if it hit her in the face. These days nothing made any sense. She wished she knew where Sally was, and if Sally knew where she was.

Lisa sat watching the door the young woman had gone through. She really didn't seem to be a prisoner. Should she just get up and walk through that door? If she could escape, should she? Whatever she might find outside could be a lot worse.

She waited a few minutes, then stood up. Slowly, one foot at a time, she stepped closer to the door. She stopped and stood in place a few minutes. She didn't want to be locked up. No. For the moment, she decided she would sit tight—until she knew her way around the house.

She walked around the room for the exercise, which seemed to loosen up her body. Lisa finally stopped at the window; all she could see was brush. There was little else about.

Lisa finally sat back down in that armchair.

She spent the whole morning in her memories, and the time went quickly. She knew that was a sign of old age. She didn't want to live in the past. She never had before and she wasn't going to start now.

She used the skirt of her dress to wipe the tears from her face.

"I have lunch ready," the young woman said as she walked back in. "Will you come to the kitchen for a change of scenery? I'll bring food to you if you don't want to come."

"Oh no, that would be just fine." The girl seemed like too much of a nice person to be part of a kidnapping. But these days, who could tell? "My dear, you need to know that my husband won't pay any money to get me back. He really does want me dead. I've decided it's all right if you kill me. I don't want to go back to that dreadful institution, or to him."

The young woman frowned compassionately. "Just follow me."

Lisa walked alongside her. They passed a dining room, then a living room. This time, all the doors were open.

"This is a small washroom," the woman said, gesturing for her to go inside. "I'll wait for you and then take you to the kitchen."

Lisa only took a few minutes. The warm water on her face felt relaxing. When she opened the door, they kept walking until they entered the kitchen.

"Mrs. Cameron, you can sit there." She pointed to a place and chair. "I don't know how to prove to you that we're not kidnapping you. If my brother hadn't taken you out of that place, you would still be there. Please, try not to think about it and enjoy your lunch. And by the way, my name is Sarah."

Lisa sat down and Sarah filled her plate with potato salad, some sliced cold meat, and a dinner roll. Then she filled a second plate and sat down across from her.

"I'm sorry, it's not elegant. In this heat, we really don't need much. I find this kitchen too warm to cook in. We're lucky that it always cools at night."

Sarah felt sorry for the old lady. She was obviously afraid and had been crying, and who could blame her?

"Oh please, this is wonderful," Lisa said. "I could pay you to let me go… Sally will look after me. I'm not sure where you can reach her…" Lisa hadn't been aware of the heat, but she suddenly felt it now. "You're right, it is warm today."

"The bedroom and sitting room both face north, where there's usually a nice cool breeze, no matter how hot it gets."

There was no way Sarah could make her understand that she hadn't been kidnapped. She hoped Peter knew what he was doing. She had no idea what to talk to this woman about, and Peter had said no conversation.

CHAPTER FIFTEEN: WHERE AM I?

"Can I tell you how much my people appreciate the help you've given us?" Sarah said, ignoring Peter's instructions to stay quiet. "I'm sure you think it's scorned, but it isn't. Sometimes it is hard to take what we already consider ours. We can only hope it will one day be made right. Our people love this country."

Sarah's thoughts often turned to history. Long ago, the Aboriginals had helped the first white people survive in a land they knew nothing about. The first white people in Saskatchewan had also been surprised to find that there were tribes settled there. The Chipewyan lived in the northern areas, the Assiniboine lived in the south, in the river valleys, and the Cree lived in the lands between the two. In the early 1900s, the railroad had brought white people here with the promise of free land that wasn't theirs to rightly give. None of that mattered to the people today, yet the Aboriginal people's heritage was rich and good. That had been the start of losing their lands and way of life.

Oh well, Sarah thought. *That's the past.*

She looked at the country today and saw what had happened to her ancestors. In a strange way, the same thing was happening all over again. A hundred years from now, she thought the white people would be fewer and another group would take the land from them.

"Please eat your lunch," Sarah said. "Peter will be furious at me for opening my mouth. I just get wrapped up in wanting to make this country better."

Sarah wasn't sure what else to say, now that she had opened her big mouth. She worried that Mrs. Cameron had misinterpreted what she'd said. The old woman had put her fork down. Was she going senile?

"Are you going to kill me when you get the money?" Lisa asked. "I really don't mind. I guess I would like you to do it when I'm sleeping, to be truthful. I've lived a good life. Had I to do it over again, I certainly would do it differently. But then, wouldn't we all?"

"Honestly, we're not kidnappers. No one is going to kill you either. You see, my brother brought you here, but I wasn't supposed to tell you that. I could get him in a lot of trouble. He's helping your niece, Sally. You do have a niece named Sally, don't you?"

"Yes, I do." Lisa looked at Sarah very carefully. "I'm not crazy or senile, you know. I've just been through so much. Those girls were trying to blackmail me for money in exchange for pictures of my husband."

Sarah froze. "I don't know anything about that. I just know my brother is working with your niece. He warned me not to talk to you, because you'll have to go on the stand in a court of law and he doesn't want me involved. I really shouldn't have said what I did. Just please believe me: we're not going to hurt you in any way."

Lisa picked up her fork again. Could she believe this woman? So much had happened and she didn't know these people. They were being nice, but just wait until they approached Hilliard. He wouldn't pay to get her back.

She heard footsteps on the hardwood floor, then looked up. Those footsteps didn't belong to the two women she knew were in the house. Who else lived here? Was it the kidnapper? She made up her mind to offer them more money than they were asking for, whatever that might be.

CHAPTER SIXTEEN
NOT A PRISONER

Blossom walked into the kitchen, smiling as she introduced the man standing next to her.

"Mrs. Cameron, this is Chief Inspector North Miller. He's here to see you."

For a moment, Lisa's head began to spin. The police had found her! She almost wished it *had* been the kidnapper.

"I will not go back to that place," Lisa insisted. "You have made a terrible mistake. I remember now that I didn't kill those girls. I'm not insane, like my husband says. Please, I need help. If you will just get my niece, she'll tell you."

The inspector walked over to the table and pulled up a chair. "Mrs. Cameron, I promise that you are never going back to that place ever again. I know you didn't kill those girls, and you're right—the police did make a dreadful mistake. I'm a friend of Sally's." He took a deep breath. "Have you finished with your lunch?"

"Mrs. Cameron didn't eat much," Sarah said, answering for her. "She's afraid of us and thinks we've kidnapped her. I tried to tell her different. Maybe you can do better than I did. Anyway, we still have dessert. Will you have some with us, Inspector?"

"That all depends on what you have."

"Wait till you see." She opened the fridge and pulled out two pieces of Saskatoon berry pie, topped with real whipped cream. She put a plate in front of both of them. "I have a special way of preparing it with brown sugar, raisins, and a touch of lemon juice. It's delicious."

"Yes, thank you." He ate a mouthful and smiled. "Absolutely wonderful. Now come on, Mrs. Cameron, you may have been raised here but no one makes pie like…" He hesitated, realizing he had made a slip "…like we do."

Lisa watched the young man dig in like he hadn't eaten in a week. He also seemed to be letting on that he and Sarah knew each other. That just added new problems. Was he a bad cop, in on the kidnapping?

Lisa took a bite and smiled. "You know, I've never grown to like these berries. I always thought they were a bit dull in taste. But this is delicious. You make a very good pie, Sarah."

"Thank you." Sarah smiled back, pleased with the compliment. She hoped the old lady wouldn't mention everything she'd said earlier, or North would be upset with her.

"Mrs. Cameron, I know how mixed-up you must be, but let me show you my badge." He handed her his wallet. "I spoke with your niece this morning. She couldn't come and also serve as your lawyer, but she knows I'm here. I asked her to give me some information that no one else knows, to prove that I'm on your side. She told me to tell you that she stayed with you once when she was sixteen and you took her out for the day. All you both did was shop and eat. You bought her several new items of clothing, including a peach-coloured angora sweater with a matching skirt and lovely cameo locket that she still cherishes to this day."

Lisa peered at him, studying his face. She so much wanted to believe him. "I've been through so much. I thought you were kidnappers, but my husband won't pay to get me back. It's a waste of time."

"I understand. Just listen to me and maybe you'll feel better." He was going to try another approach, even more friendly, to get her confidence. Obviously she had made up her mind that she had been kidnapped. "First, I want you to understand that whatever you tell me is strictly between us. I have to keep you here for your own safety, until we have the killer behind bars. Like your niece, truth is very important to me, too."

"That does sound like Sally. You mean that you're working with her now?"

"Yes, Mrs. Cameron, and we have several good leads on the killer. We have to fill in a few missing pieces, however, and that's where I need your help. I need you to tell me exactly what happened when you went into that apartment, the day the girls were killed."

She went on to explain what she remembered. It was the same story she'd told Sally earlier.

"You see, there were nights when my husband stayed late at the courthouse to clean up matters he'd been too busy to cope with," Lisa added. "He would sleep on the sofa in his office. There were other excuses. He would work late, or catch up on his reading, or relax at the club and stay the night… Well, those were all lies. You see, I'm finally facing up to reality. I guess he spent those nights with Judith or Clare or some other woman. I really didn't know he had such an appetite for women. Believe it or not, this was a side of him I never saw. Or maybe I just dismissed it. When he was gone those nights, my housekeeper Anna and I felt secure knowing we had a gun close by."

North nodded, taking notes of all this. "And how about your family finances?"

"I always received an allowance from my father, before he passed away. I gave a lot of it to my husband, and the rest went into my personal account. My father had insisted that I keep the money in an account in my own name. He never knew that I gave some of it to Hilliard, but Hilliard looked after all the household bills."

"And when you gave money to Corey, where did that money come from?"

"From my personal account. Mind you, Hilliard paid her as well. We both paid, not knowing the other was doing the same thing. Corey was a chain about our necks. I'm sorry. I wish I could feel differently, now that she's dead. But I'm partially to blame. I should never have paid her in the first place."

"Mrs. Cameron, what business was your father in?"

"Oil, on both sides of the border."

"And when did he die?"

"Ten years ago. Of course, I inherited his fortune."

"So you became a great deal richer with his death. I don't mean that in any way as a reproach. But I presume you could have gone on paying the blackmail if you had wanted to."

"Yes, I am very wealthy. Don't judge me as stingy, though. I give a lot away, some to people who have needs and never know where it comes from. I help wherever there's a need, if I know about it. Oil keeps coming from the ground, so I do fine."

North suddenly thought of another angle. If Judge Cameron could declare her to be insane, he might inherit her money. And with the girls dead, he wouldn't have to pay them anymore."

"Mrs. Cameron, if something should happen to you, who inherits your wealth?"

"You'd be surprised," she said, smiling mischievously. "I knew that when I inherited my father's money, it had to go where it would do the most good. All I'll say for now is that my husband was never going to get my money."

CHAPTER SIXTEEN: NOT A PRISONER

"Mrs. Cameron, thank you so much for being straight with me." He closed his notebook. "Sally wants to see you very badly. We just think that it's better if she doesn't know where you are for now. If she has to defend you, it'll count against her to have been involved in this little escapade. She could even lose her licence to practice law. So please keep a low profile and accept my sister's hospitality for a few more days."

So that's the connection! Lisa thought. *Sarah and the inspector are siblings.*

"I have one other thing to talk to you about," North said. "Sally has arranged for a really good friend to come and see you. He's a special doctor who can say in court that you're in your right mind. He has excellent credentials. Will you talk to him and just be yourself?"

"Yes, of course I will. I want so much to clear my name of this nonsense."

"Good. He'll be here sometime today." He stood up, stretching. "I'll be back, I promise. May I walk you back to your room? Maybe a rest would be in order."

"Thank you, I'm very tired. The stress is strenuous."

North took her arm, just like a real gentleman, and ushered to the bedroom for a nap. Lisa watched him leave, thinking what a nice young man he was.

I wonder if he's married, Lisa thought. *Sally could use a nice young man like that.*

Lisa lay in bed, thinking that she had better do exactly what she had been told so far. At least for the time being, she seemed safe. They didn't appear to be the bad guys. That small, shiny licence had looked like a real cop's badge. She had to believe he wasn't working for her husband.

In no time, Lisa had dozed off. But the next thing she knew, she was being awakened by Sarah.

"I don't want you to sleep too long or you won't be able to sleep tonight," Sarah explained. "How about a quick face wash and some tea and cookies?"

Several minutes later, she was alone in the sitting room again.

She noticed that a table had been set up, and there was a jigsaw puzzle sitting in a box right in the middle of the table. Good! Something to occupy her time and make the day go by quicker. She smiled when she looked at the picture on the front of the box: a skyline of Toronto. It had to be from Sally. She felt much better.

Sarah walked back into the room, carrying a tray.

"After having to put up with my brother for an hour, you must be more than ready for some refreshment." She set the tray down on a TV table in front of her. "Now help yourself to the cookies. And the tea is hot, so be careful."

Lisa stood up after she'd finished the snack, with the tray in her hands, and walked out of the sitting room. Not sure which way to go, she chose left, hoping to end up in the kitchen. Instead she found herself among the bedrooms and knew she had gone the wrong way. She turned around, still confused.

She soon ended up in the doorway to the kitchen. Inside, she heard a voice coming from the television: "The police are expecting a breakthrough in their investigation into the recent murder of two young women. Sources say that an arrest in this case is imminent. As we learn more, we'll bring that news to you. Now, back to our regular programming."

Sarah was the only person in the kitchen as Lisa entered.

"Where would you like me to put these things?" Lisa asked.

"Right in the sink would be great," Sarah said. "I wash by hand and water is precious out here. We're on wells and have to be careful what we use. Sometimes I think the prairie is like the desert, only no sand—all gumbo."

A moment later, the doorbell rang.

CHAPTER SIXTEEN: NOT A PRISONER

"It's all right," Sarah said. "I think that's the doctor, here to speak with you. I'll go answer the door and make sure he is who he's supposed to be. Stay back here, just in case."

Soon Sarah walked back into the room with a smiling man.

"Mrs. Cameron, I'm Sam," he said. "I'm a doctor of psychology and a good friend of your niece, Sally. I'm here to make an assessment for the courts, if necessary, to prove that you're healthy. Sarah, if you'll leave this lovely lady with me, we'll talk for a bit and then I'll get out of your way." The doctor handed Lisa a sealed envelope. "Please open it, Mrs. Cameron. You'll see that it's a note from Sally."

Lisa did as he said. She read the note three times, then handed it back to him.

"I have to burn it, so no one can use it against your niece in court," Sam said. "She's not supposed to know where you are. She actually doesn't, thanks to Peter and some good friends."

Already he could see that he was going to like Lisa.

Over the course of the next four hours, they spoke about the possibility of her husband being the killer. They discussed about how she would react if that was proven. They also talked about the divorce she wanted from her husband and how she planned on starting a new life on her own.

By the time they were finished, Lisa felt so much better. She thanked him for coming to see her.

She had to admit that since she had come here, she certainly had met some very nice people. She was exhausted when he left and had a nap in her chair. She awoke sometime later feeling much better.

CHAPTER SEVENTEEN
MAN TROUBLE

Another day was about to start, and Sally hadn't been to bed yet. The last two weeks had gone by very quickly. It seemed unbelievable. Since coming to the bed-and-breakfast, she had managed to elude people by climbing into the rental car at the back of the house and constantly ensuring that they weren't followed.

She sat on the side of her bed, staring at the cascading moonbeams, drifting and sparkling specks of dust, and the dancing shafts of light from the window. Her mind was lost in thought.

She had her shower, cleaned her teeth, and brushed her long, thick blond hair. She had worn it in a French braid all day, making it neat and cool. But now it was untidy and full of kinks. It had been very hot today.

She looked at her watch, which she'd lain on the side table, and saw that it was two-thirty in the morning. While she was exhausted and really needed to crawl under the floral sheets and go to never never land, she wasn't sleepy.

There heard a soft knock on her door. It opened and Slipper walked in.

"I can't seem to get to sleep, and I noticed your light was still on," Slipper said. "How are you doing?"

"Much the same."

CHAPTER SEVENTEEN: MAN TROUBLE

Sally looked at Slipper's feet and chuckled. "Those fuzzy bunnies have big ears. I like your slippers—and to think they match Almira's! That must have taken some planning."

"Very funny. They're cute, don't you think?" Slipper sighed. "We're overtired and have too much on our minds to sleep. Are you in the mood to listen as I run some very personal thoughts by you? I need some advice about a man, oh you of great wisdom."

"Great wisdom, that's a laugh. With two men in my life and all my other problems, I'm probably of little use to you."

Slipper sat on the bed next to Sally, stretching her legs and leaning into the pile of cushions at their backs.

"I have a problem I never would have believed possible a year ago," Slipper said. "Even though I've only known you a short time, I feel like we've become good friends. I know that what I say will stay with you. Sally, I really miss my husband and that's unusual for me. North Miller and I worked together as partners for several years, on and off. It was strictly friendship between us, but my problem now is that I've been working too many hours with North. I want it to be more. When North comes into the room, my heart beats a little faster. He makes me feel young and alive, something I never get from my husband."

Sally let her talk, knowing she didn't have the answers.

"You have to understand, Conn is a good husband. He's a great cop as well and loves every minute of his police work. But our marriage feels like it's lasted fifty years, not just fifteen. The more I think about it, the more I realize we're both bored with each other. Maybe the truth is that neither of us is really happy anymore. Maybe we need some time apart. Still, I honestly doubt our marriage can be repaired. I think this is something we've been ignoring, hoping it would go away and it won't. I think we both feel the same way.

"Anyway, there's a lot of silly things happening. Like when dinnertime arrived this evening, I phoned for takeout Chinese food. You say, so what? Do you know what a treat that was? Conn would never bring in something like that. He says my cooking is too good to eat restaurant food. Tonight, all three of us, including North, dug in, and it was delicious and fun. Conn would have hated it, and that's just one of many things. Do you see?"

Sally didn't know what to say. Did couples get bored with each other after a while? Maybe they just settled into a routine, forgetting what was going on around them. That sounded like her and Mark, and they weren't even married yet.

"I honestly don't know what to say," Sally said. "Have you thought of marriage counselling?"

"Sally, you have to face the same question. I see the way you and Peter look at each other. Just between you and me, there's a lot going on there, and don't just say it's all in my head. It's there. Can you just ignore it?"

Sally bunched the pillows behind her, trying to get more comfortable. "You're not telling me something I don't already know. I can't explain how very safe I feel with Peter. I don't trust men easily, and then along comes Peter. It makes no sense to me at all. He and I haven't known each other long."

"I'll tell you something, Sally Cameron: you're as mixed-up as I am." They both looked at each other and laughed again. "The one thing you can be thankful for is that you don't have that piece of paper binding you to Mark like I do to Conn. Without that document, I would be with North." Slipper let out a sigh. "I'm going to bed. See you in a few hours."

Sally watched her leave the room, smiling to herself. Thinking about their talk, she tucked herself into bed, enjoying the nice smell of lavender among the sheets. She stretched out long and tall, and after a few minutes, slightly curled up and tucking her hands to the side of her head, she fell asleep.

CHAPTER EIGHTEEN
AN UNEXPECTED TURN OF EVENTS

When the alarm clock chimed, Sally still felt a little dozy. She hadn't had enough hours of sleep, with so much conversation the previous night. She and Slipper would both pay for it today.

Sally made her way to the breakfast table and found Slipper already there, smiling at her as she sat down.

"What a night I had," Slipper said. "One nightmare after another. Sometimes they seemed so real! I swear I feel like I haven't slept at all."

Sally groaned. "I know exactly what you mean."

Martha swept into the kitchen holding the phone. "There's a call for you, Slipper."

What now? Sally wondered as Slipper took the receiver.

"Yes?" Slipper answered. She listened for a while, then said "All right" and gave Sally the thumbs-up sign. "That was one of those calls that's both good and bad news. It's great news for you, though. Your aunt has been given a clean bill of health, which has been reported to the police. Now for the bad news: unless you or the police find another suspect in the murders, the case will go to court and she could be sent to prison. North wants to keep her hidden until the killer is found and all charges can be dropped."

That made Sally very nervous. They still had a lot of work to do.

"Now get this," Slipper continued. "North talked to your uncle about Dr. Feldman's report, and he apparently said he was very pleased, that he's known all along that she was innocent. Can you believe it? Then he asked when she would be coming home!"

They sat in silence for a while at the kitchen table, both lost in their own thoughts as they processed all this news.

"About last night," Slipper said. "I'm going to sit down and have a good talk with Conn. If he will be truthful, maybe our marriage does have a chance. At this point, I honestly don't know."

Sally nodded. "Give yourself time. Everything will work out all right."

"Thanks for listening. I've needed to get that out for some time. There aren't a lot of people I can talk to."

They both stood up and hugged.

"All right," Slipper said. "Where to today, Ms. Cameron?"

"I want to go to the office of Peter's newspaper. Not to see him, but to check out some old editions."

"Right."

Together, they walked out the back door and climbed into the rental car. Once off the main highway, they headed toward the north end of the city.

As they drove through downtown, Slipper's eyes noticed a light green car in the rear-view mirror. She suddenly had the sense that something awful was about to happen. Her heart pounded as they watched the suspicious vehicle, which had been following them for quite a while.

You're probably just being paranoid, she thought. *The cops have stopped following you. Sure, there are still reporters who want a story, but they certainly don't pose a threat. And yet...*

CHAPTER EIGHTEEN: AN UNEXPECTED TURN OF EVENTS

After a few minutes, she decided to make a random right turn at the next street. Her eyes stayed on the mirror, one hand on her stomach and the other on the steering wheel. This was crazy. She had been in all kind of dangerous situations and never reacted like this.

Indeed, the green car turned as well. She made another quick turn, reminding herself that her gun was still in its holster, ready if she needed it.

"Why in the world are we driving in circles?" Sally asked. Then she noticed that Slipper was watching something in the rear-view mirror, and Slipper had placed her gun on the console between them. "What's the matter? Haven't we gone off the beaten path?"

"I think we have a tail," Slipper said. "A very suspicion one and someone a little stupid. Certainly not a professional tail. If I didn't know better, I might think he wants me to know he's there. It may be a reporter, although I have a bad feeling about this one."

Sally could feel the tension coming from Slipper. She had never seen her so worried.

"I guess it could be a coincidence." Slipper carried on driving, keeping an even speed. "Somehow I don't think it is."

This wasn't good. The driver of that car was keeping far enough back that she couldn't see who was behind the wheel.

It was time for a showdown.

"Sally, I'm going to pull over." Looking ahead, she saw the same boutique store Sally had shopped in a few days ago. That could prove a good use of the next few minutes of Sally's time. "I want to see who's in that car, so I'm going to park and I want you to go into that boutique store you visited on the weekend. The other driver will probably park, and then he and I are going to get better acquainted. Don't come out of the store until I come and get you. Trust me, this is the cop in me. I know what I'm doing."

"Why don't we just call North?" Sally asked.

Slipper was still watching the car, which was moving too slowly. "I hate to bother North if it isn't anything to be concerned about."

She wished that was all it was but knew it wasn't. She needed Sally to be safe inside. Judge Cameron was still the enemy, and this city certainly had a few hitmen for hire.

"I thought we agreed that these attempts on my life were strictly scare tactics," Sally said. "Surely he wouldn't really harm me."

In all truthfulness, Sally thought he might. She had been threatening him, after all, and now she almost seemed to be involved in her aunt's divorce.

Slipper sighed. "Maybe I'm just being paranoid, but please do as I ask. I just have a feeling about this."

"All right, be careful. You've become a good friend and I don't want anything happening to you. I still think we should call North."

"I can look after myself."

Slipper pulled up to the curb right in front of the store. Sally was just about to leave the car when the green car pulled up right beside them. A shot rang out, then another, and Sally screamed.

Slipper slumped over in her seat, blood everywhere.

Before Sally knew what she was doing, her instinct took control and she grabbed for Slipper's phone and dialled 911. She had a lot of blood on her as she cradled Slipper in her arms. She'd been shot—and badly.

Sally just hung on to her friend, repeating the same thing over and over: "No, no, no, no... Slipper, please breathe. Keep fighting. I need you." Her words rang out in anguish.

The next thing Sally knew, she was crying and being examined, then lifted out of the car. The emergency workers had to pry her arms from Slipper. There were ambulances and police cruisers

CHAPTER EIGHTEEN: AN UNEXPECTED TURN OF EVENTS

everywhere. Yet for some reason, nothing seemed real. She couldn't think. It was like her mind shut down.

North crouched down next to her as they loaded Sally into an ambulance.

"Is Slipper all right?" Sally asked.

Peter arrived at that moment. Devastated, he clung to Sally, getting blood all over him.

The paramedics did everything they could to get the two men out of the way as they worked on the women.

North wouldn't leave Slipper's side, and finally one of the paramedics had to pull him away, comforting the inspector in his arms while he cried. Obviously this young man had loved the woman very much.

"Relax, Sally, everything is going to be all right," Peter said into her ear. "You've been shot. The paramedics have hooked you up to an IV, to relax you. My darling, I love you, and I will get whoever did this. I promise."

In a daze, Sally heard a whistle as though from a great distance. She knew it was the sound of the ambulance she was in, and Peter was right there with her.

The world turned grey, and then there was nothing but blackness.

*　*　*

Over the next three hours, the little hospital waiting room filled with people, including Chief Markell, Peter, North, and even the city's mayor. News of the shooting had travelled fast, although the police had issued a statement that nothing would be verified to the press—no names, no details. Unfortunately, the shooting had taken place on a busy street with lots of witnesses.

The hospital had called Conn, who showed up at the hospital looking for North. Conn wanted a firsthand account of what had happened, so North told him everything he knew, which was very little. Conn was furious, more so that Slipper had been working. He had always hated her working.

Peter was pacing in circles. No matter what North said, he wouldn't sit down.

"If anything happens to Sally, I'll kill the person who did this," Peter remarked over and over.

In his anguish, Peter didn't even notice North's own suffering.

Finally, after two hours the doctors arrived in the waiting room and spoke first to Conn. He then left the hospital immediately, choosing not to go down and see his wife in the morgue, where she had been taken for the police to look for more evidence about the shooter. The doctors explained that several bullets had riddled her body, only they put it much more nicely than that.

Conn cried when he thought about Slipper. He had loved her for fifteen years and didn't know what had gone so wrong between them. Now he had lost her and he would give anything to have her back. He dared not think ahead to the funeral he would have to arrange.

Next, the doctors approached North, as the police officer in charge of the investigation, and explained the situation: Slipper had died instantly.

I'm going to die, North thought in the moment. *I can't hear these words. This was the woman I loved.*

He sat down, not even looking at the doctor. The doctor was surprised at how emotional he was—far more emotional even than the woman's husband.

"The other woman, Sally Cameron, was lucky. The two bullets that hit her weren't life-threatening. She had one bullet in her left shoulder and another in the upper arm, same side. We operated

CHAPTER EIGHTEEN: AN UNEXPECTED TURN OF EVENTS

to get the bullets out, and she's in recovery now. It'll be some time before she wakes up." The doctor paused. "I'm no pathologist, although I'm fairly sure it's no fault of the shooter that she isn't dead, too. They'll have to investigate the scene further to find out who was meant to be the victim. We also don't know if the shooter was driving at the time. Ms. Cameron may be able to tell us, when she's awake."

North knew that forensics would have to go over the scene to be able to tell what had really happened, but his instinct told him that this had been an amateur shooting, with the shooter opening fire and letting the bullets go where they might.

"Ms. Cameron may not remember what happened because of shock," the doctor warned him. "She'll be here for a few days."

North turned just as his partner, Detective Norm Walters, suddenly appeared in the waiting room. He put his hand on North's shoulder and steered him aside where what they said wouldn't be overheard.

"Sorry about Slipper, man," he said quietly. "She loved you. Always remember that." He hesitated, knowing that he had to get down to business now. "The shooter managed to drive off. It all happened so quickly. Two people who were standing on the sidewalk were able to give us a few numbers from the license plate of a light green car that sped away. We have all their statements, and we're looking for the shooter now."

North looked up, realizing that three others officers had arrived to offer whatever help they could.

* * *

Five hours later, Sally was brought to a private room where Peter and North were waiting, one on either side of the bed. They watched over her sleeping form, looking at each other from time to time. Peter knew that North must have mixed feelings. After all, Sally was alive and Slipper was dead. He hadn't even realized at first that Slipper and North had been in love.

One question hung over the room: should Sally's uncle be informed? What if he had done it? Aside from Lisa, he was her only relative here in Regina. As next of kin, they decided that he should know what had happened.

As they waited for Judge Cameron's arrival at the hospital, North was anxious to see his reaction to the news.

CHAPTER NINETEEN
THE HOSPITAL

North made up his mind that there wouldn't be another attempt on Sally's life, so he stationed a cop to stand at her door. He didn't want to accuse Judge Cameron of the shooting, simply because of who he was, so his hands were tied for the time being. But North insisted that the police put a tail on the judge, just in case.

"I wish Sally would wake up before her uncle arrives," Peter said, looking from North to Sally and back again.

Suddenly, her eyes opened. Then they closed.

Peter gripped her hand. "Sally, are you awake?"

She opened her eyes again. "Peter," she whispered.

"You have no idea how happy I am to see those beautiful eyes."

She smiled and wet her lips with her tongue. "Dry."

North handed Peter a glass of ice water from the table on his side of the bed. He let Sally sip some water. She had trouble swallowing it, so he wet her lips with his finger.

Sitting at the edge of his seat, Peter thought she looked awful. But they needed her to talk, to tell them if she had seen the shooter.

She turned her head and saw North. "Hi."

North smiled back. "Good to see you looking awake. Don't strain yourself. You've been in that operating room getting a bullet removed, but you're okay now."

Sally tried to move her head, although it hurt. Besides, her shoulder bandage was in the way. She looked about, realizing she was indeed in a hospital.

"What happened? Why am I here?" Her voice was soft and a bit wispy. "Peter, why has North been crying?"

She was confused. The police officer's cheeks were wet with tears.

"You gave us a scare, you know," Peter said. "We're just worried about you, you idiot. We're soft-hearted."

"Someone shot me?" she asked.

"Yes. It isn't something to worry about now. You'll have a sore shoulder and arm for a while." Peter realized there was no point in asking her anything right now. She obviously didn't remember what had happened.

For the next two hours, she was in and out of consciousness. No one said anything to her about Slipper.

Meanwhile, Judge Cameron came by while Sally slept and Peter hid in the washroom. He only stayed a few minutes before leaving again.

When North asked later, Sally couldn't remember anything about the car or the shooter. For that matter, she couldn't even remember being in the car at all.

The nurse's station soon received a call from Sally's father, which North took, and then another call from Sally's fiancé, Mark Trotter, who insisted that he would be on the next plane out.

Peter was determined to fight for the woman he loved, but North had talked him out of it. He reminded Peter that the ball was in Sally's court.

Both North and Peter stayed the night, sitting in chairs and sleeping at Sally's side. They dozed off and on, waking every time she made a sound only to find her still asleep. The nurse told them she would be a hundred times better in the morning.

CHAPTER NINETEEN: THE HOSPITAL

They had coffee and doughnuts brought to them by one of the officers stationed outside. When they finished, the door opened again and a sergeant poked his head in.

"The nurse says that two men are coming upstairs now, a Willard Cameron and a Chief Inspector Mark Trotter from Toronto."

The sergeant then left again, closing the door behind him.

"Stay, Peter," North said. "You might as well meet them."

"Another time. North, don't leave her side." His look was also well interpreted. Peter kissed Sally and smiled. "I dare you to compare."

North shook his head back and forth as Peter slipped off into the linen closet next door.

Just then, a tall, sternly good-looking man walked in. For a minute, North was shaken. He could have sworn it was Sally's uncle! Behind him was another tall man, only much younger. Both men walked over to the bed, totally ignoring North.

"Sally, my sweet darling girl," the younger man said, sitting beside her, taking her hand, and gently kissing her. "Can you hear me?"

The love was there for anyone to see. North was glad now that Peter had left. This would have broken Peter's heart.

North knew all about broken hearts.

"Do you know what that call was like, to hear you were shot?" the young man asked. "I've been worried out of my mind."

Sally's eyes opened. "Peter?" She then focused on the young man, registering surprise. "Mark, what are you doing here? You shouldn't have come. I'm just fine." She turned her head as best she could. "North, where's Slipper? I remember she was covered in blood. How is she?"

Mark didn't let the inspector answer. "Sally, we've been worried about you. Why would someone want to shoot you? It makes no sense."

Mark then looked to her father, who was also in shock. How could this happen?

"Dad," Sally said, a puzzled look coming over her face. "You came with Mark?"

Her father bent down and kissed her cheek. Before he could say anything, however, two nurses bustled into the room.

"If you gentlemen will excuse us, I need to check my patient," one nurse said. "She needs a painkiller, among a few other things. She's really in no condition to be talking and having so many visitors. If you're that concerned, I suggest getting out of here and letting us do our work. I'll let you know when we're done."

All the men walked out into the hall. North noticed that he was certainly given the once-over by both visitors.

"I believe you must be Chief Inspector Mark Trotter," North said. "Sally speaks of you all the time. I'm North Miller, with the local police. I've been looking after your lady, since she's had several threats on her life recently. This one totally surprised us."

Mark nodded. "I understand from the guard on duty that you're my counterpart here in Regina." He gestured to the older man. "This is Sally's father, Judge Willard Cameron."

North and the judge exchanged pleasantries.

"Inspector, can you tell us what happened and how Sally came to be shot?" Sally's father asked.

The words sounded cold coming from him. It made North take a second look at this man. He already hadn't liked him, and now even less so. This man wasn't any better than his brother.

"I think the nurses are going to be a while," North said. "If you'll come down to the cafeteria, we can get a coffee and I can fill you in." He took a moment to study the older man's face more closely. "What a surprise it is that you look so much like your brother. Sally told me you were twins, but you really are very much alike."

CHAPTER NINETEEN: THE HOSPITAL

"We haven't changed over the years," the judge said. "We've just grown older. I can't understand how Sally became mixed up in my sister-in-law's trouble. My brother begged her to go home and she sure has a stubborn side. Maybe this will teach her a lesson: to listen when her family know best—"

"If you don't mind, we'd appreciate going for coffee," Mark interrupted. "Sally has a way of picking up trouble, and she keeps me on my toes. But it sounds like you've replaced me on this trip and I do appreciate you looking out for her."

North didn't reply as they took the elevator downstairs. He hoped Peter would have a little time with her before they returned to the room.

Once North had gotten them coffees, the three men sat down at a table in the hospital's cafeteria.

"Ms. Cameron has taken two bullets," North began. He went on to describe her injuries and the surgery that had been performed. He held up a hand, preventing the other men from asking questions as he kept going. "The woman who died was Slipper McKinnon, her bodyguard and a part-time police officer. She took most of the bullets…" His voice caught in his throat. "Sorry, we worked together as partners for a few years and I cared about her a great deal."

North trailed off, noticing the shock on the men's faces.

"You need to know that she was a marvellous person and really cared for Sally." North's voice broke again. "Excuse me a minute." He took out his handkerchief and blew into it. Afterward, his voice strengthened again. "Slipper saved Sally's life."

He spent the next twenty minutes answering as many questions as he dared, but he didn't accuse Sally's uncle or go into details of the police investigation. It was difficult to answer questions since Sally's dad and uncle were so deeply involved.

It didn't take long for North to see that Mark loved Sally very much.

Mark was more than curious about everything he'd heard. The personal way this inspector used his fiancée's first name made him think the two were well-acquainted with each other.

After their talk, the three men returned upstairs to Sally's room. They arrived just as another young man was leaving.

"Who was that?" Mark asked. "He doesn't look like a doctor."

North was saved from having to answer when a nurse came out of the room.

"Actually, gentlemen, Ms. Cameron will be asleep in about five minutes," the nurse said. "I suggest you leave her and visit again after lunch. She needs her rest."

North was about to walk away down the hall when he noticed Mark looking over his shoulder, not wanting to leave.

"Believe me, Inspector Trotter, she needs her sleep," North said. "We have hopes that she'll remember seeing the shooter once she recovers."

"Yes, you're right." Mark looked at North. "I'll only be a moment."

Mark walked quickly back into Sally's room and saw that she was sleeping. He leaned over and gave her a kiss.

"I love you," he whispered.

North dropped Mark and her father off at the Hotel Saskatchewan. He watched him pass through the front door before pulling away from the curb to park a few feet away. His suspicions had been right. Within five minutes, Mark came back out of the building. North watched as the man hailed a cab and gave the driver some money.

Mark was making his way back to Sally.

* * *

CHAPTER NINETEEN: THE HOSPITAL

At the hospital, Mark walked up to the nurse's station and showed the officer there his badge.

"Do you mind waiting a minute?" the officer asked.

Mark watched as the officer walked down the hall toward Sally's room and stepped inside.

In the room, the officer made eye contact with Peter. "You might consider leaving," he said to Peter. "The fiancé is here again."

"Can he do that?" Peter asked in a soft voice, almost a whisper.

"The nurse has no objections. He's her fiancé, after all."

"Okay, I'll leave." Peter reached over and kissed her. She seemed to respond, although she wasn't fully awake.

Peter then followed the officer out the door.

"Who are you?" Mark asked Peter when they ran into each other in the hallway. He seemed surprised to see this same guy coming out of Sally's room.

"Oh, excuse me," Peter said. "I just came to make sure everything's all right. Until we catch the shooter, we have to keep close watch."

Peter figured this might make Mark assume he was a cop.

"You're very conscientious in your work, wouldn't you say?" There was no mistaking the look of anger that glistened on Mark's face as he spoke.

Peter just smiled and walked away. *Inspector Trotter, you're going to see a lot of me if you stay around here.*

CHAPTER TWENTY
RELEASE

The shift was about to change as North arrived back at the hospital, so he decided it made a good excuse for him to check on Sally.

He walked upstairs, then opened the door and entered Sally's room.

"Inspector Trotter, that night went quickly," he said to Mark, who sat at Sally's bedside. He hoped this man hadn't run into Peter.

Mark nodded, not saying anything for a moment. The night before, through a crack in the door, he had witnessed a kiss between Peter and Sally. Peter had looked very much like a man in love with his girl. Who was this man, and how did he fit in? Inspector Miller seemed to know him well.

Sally, have you fallen in love with someone else while I was away? he thought to himself.

He turned his attention back to Sally, not caring what the inspector thought.

"Sally, I love you more than life," he said softly. "I couldn't live without you, doll."

"Mark." She smiled as she opened her eyes. "I know. I'm so tired. They have me drugged for pain. Have you met North? He has the same job as you do back home. He's not only a cop, but a really good friend. I don't know what I would have done without him and his friend Peter."

Peter, Mark thought, remembering that Sally had said that name earlier. *That must be the other guy's name.*

"Yes, I've met Inspector Miller. I've only seen the other man coming or going."

"I'm glad you did. Was it a good flight here?"

"Not bad at all, other than that I had a seat right next to your father."

"I'm confused. Who called you?"

"After the shooting, the chief of police called your father, who then called me. We caught the first plane out."

"Oh." She looked about the room, wondering where Peter had gone. "My father shouldn't have come. I don't want to talk to him again. North, has he spoken to my uncle yet?"

Mark sighed. "Sally, no matter what has gone on between you, the man loves you. He means well."

"Everything is all right, Sally," North said. "You need to relax so you can get back to looking after your aunt's case, remember?"

"Wait a minute," Mark objected. "Her health is more important than her aunt's case right now."

She shook her head weakly. "No, Mark, you don't know what has gone on here. North is right. Take Father back home. I don't want him here. I can't explain now, but I love you, and you two are better off in Toronto. I have some loose ends to tie up before I go back."

Mark sighed, then leaned in and whispered in her ear, "We're two of a kind, doll. Don't you desert me."

"I won't, Mark. It's just that I have to see this through."

After being there all morning, Mark reluctantly left to go for lunch.

Within minutes, Peter was back.

"I have to know about Slipper," Sally told him. "I know she was shot, because I had the blood on my hands. Peter, she's become my best friend, even more than a sister to me. I'm afraid to ask what's happened, but is the reason you're not talking about her because she's dead?"

Peter didn't say anything, and that was enough. She knew. He sat on the end of the bed, reached out, and took Sally's hand. She fell into his arms and cried, tears rolling down her face. He did his best to comfort her. He loved her so much.

North came into the room, saw what was going on, then turned and went back out into the hallway. He wasn't sure if he would ever be able to face Slipper's death, but he doubted it.

"Slipper died instead of me," Sally said, cradled in Peter's arms. "North must be taking this very badly. Poor North. Slipper loved him, you know. Maybe it's better this way for both of them. If I could only do it over again, maybe this wouldn't have happened. Peter, when is the funeral?"

"Sally, whoever had been in that car with you would have been killed. It just happened to be Slipper. The person who fired that gun must be crazy. Anyway, the police are holding the body for a few days. They will probably release it next week."

She let out a loud sob. "Who did this?"

"We don't know. There were a lot of witnesses with different stories. But we'll find the truth, you can bet your life on that." Peter pulled back from the embrace. "Life is complicated at times, isn't it? North loved Slipper and she had a husband."

"It isn't that easy," she said. "I would have wanted whatever she wanted for herself."

Looking up into his eyes, Sally wanted to cry again. But she held her lips tight and refused to give in to this form of weakness.

Suddenly, Peter stood. "I'm sorry, I have to go to work."

CHAPTER TWENTY: RELEASE

Sally watched the door close and wondered why life had to be so complex. Was there ever a right way? Who could say what way she should go? She closed her eyes, and in a few minutes the pills she had taken before breakfast snapped into effect. She lay down and finally napped.

* * *

The next five days were busy ones that kept North up to his ears in work. Sally would be getting out of the hospital tomorrow and she seemed quite well. When she returned home, she was to see about some therapy on her shoulder and neck.

Her father had visited once more and then gone back to Toronto. They hadn't discussed one word about either her aunt or uncle. Not only that, but North had learned that Sally's father had only spoken to his brother once while he was in town—over the phone from his hotel—and they had said nothing about the murders.

Mark knew that Sally would never fly home until she had wrapped up this case. She had become her own judge now, with a vengeance for finding the killer. She wouldn't let the shooter scare her away. Fear? Oh yes. No doubt she quaked in her boots at the prospect of going out on the streets again. But Mark knew this was Sally, and no one would discourage her.

Mark didn't once mention what he had seen Peter do. After all, he loved and trusted Sally, and all he wanted was for her to be happy. He didn't believe deep in his heart that she would be happy with anyone other than himself. That wasn't being conceited; he just knew Sally.

Nonetheless, he caught the next flight home.

* * *

Sally wanted to walk out of the hospital on her own two feet, but the nurse insisted on wheeling her to the back entrance in a wheelchair. Her new police bodyguard, a man named Warren, went out the door first to check the area. When he determined that everything was fine, Sally was escorted to a rental car, which was parked and waiting at the curb. She smiled at him as he helped her into the back seat beside yet another new bodyguard, Avery.

Before they left, Peter explained that it was still important that they not be seen together. But once this was over, he teased that he was going to take out a full page ad in the paper with a picture of him kissing her right on the lips. Then people could think whatever they wanted.

Peter stayed behind, letting Warren drive the car away.

As they drove, Sally got a closer look at Avery. Peter had told her that he had a nickname on the police force: Hulk. She thought the name suited him perfectly. He was a very large man, taller than six feet and muscled. He reminded her of those huge wrestlers she sometimes saw on TV while flipping channels.

Sally felt suddenly frightened as they turned onto the street. She had to take several deep breaths to control her emotions.

"You know, the car that was following us was light green," Sally said, wondering if the police knew this detail. "I should have told Peter."

Avery smiled at her. "We have a witness who already told us that, and she thought the driver was a woman, too. We've got some good leads."

"A woman! I suppose that's possible. She meant to kill me, didn't she? That means we're back to Clare or Judith as suspects."

"Yes, and that's why we have to be careful. Although this doesn't mean that the girls' killer was a woman, too. And there could have been someone else in the car with her."

Sally looked at the large man, hoping he didn't see how frightened she was just to be riding in this car. She did her best not to look out the windows. She wondered if she would ever feel safe again. She couldn't defend herself against guns! She had been so sure she could look after herself, but she had been proven wrong.

She shifted in the seat, trying to get more comfortable, but every movement hurt.

"Look, guys, I've been thinking," she said. "I want to go and see my uncle. How I'm going to handle that, I have no idea. Sometimes coming right to the point is the only way. I'm fairly good at discerning the truth and questioning people. I intend to put him right on the spot."

Warren shook his head from the driver's seat. "Peter told us to take you straight to the bed-and-breakfast. Ma'am, maybe you should consider resting some more or you'll end up right back in the hospital. Believe me, your uncle isn't going anywhere. You're stuffed full of painkillers at the moment."

"Sorry, you're right. The problem is, I'm not a sit-around, do-nothing kind of gal."

To Sally, this was just another day and she still had a lot of work to do. She needed to keep busy, to take her mind off her own aches and pains.

CHAPTER TWENTY-ONE
DECISION TIME

Warren pulled up to the bed-and-breakfast just as Sally opened her eyes from a short nap.

"We're here," he said. "You were lost in another world there, but now it's time to come back to this one—not that it's so great right now."

She would so much rather have gone to Peter's, but she agreed this was best for now.

Peter had phoned ahead and Martha had prepared a light lunch for them, even arranging a place for the two men to sleep there in the room Slipper had occupied. Lunch consisted of toasted egg salad sandwiches with tomato slices, potato chips, and carrots and celery sticks. There was rice pudding, with raisins and cinnamon, for dessert.

She couldn't believe how starved she was, and her food disappeared very quickly. Because tension still clouded her mind, she took a couple of pain pills afterward and took another nap.

When Sally finally opened her eyes again, daylight was shining through the windows. It was two-thirty in the afternoon and she had so much to do. She sat on the side of the bed and took a few deep breaths. She couldn't raise her arms like normal or do her usual stretches; it was too painful. Her shoulder was still bandaged.

CHAPTER TWENTY-ONE: DECISION TIME

She headed for the washroom and washed her face in good warm water, then brushed her thick hair and quickly wrapped it into a bun at the back of her neck. She wanted to look professional when she saw her uncle.

This meeting might be one of the worst things she would ever have to do.

Sally walked into the kitchen where Avery handed her a cup of hot coffee.

"Two heaping spoonfuls of sugar and black," Avery said. "We just finished brewing a new pot."

"Thanks. Do you think Martha will mind if we take it with us? I slept like a rock." She stood up straight and faced him. "I have to go see my uncle. As much as I'm dreading this, it has to be done. Do you know the address?"

"Yes, ma'am. I mentioned to Inspector Miller that you wanted to go, and he says he will meet us there. He'll wait outside during the meeting, since he doesn't want Judge Cameron to be aware that he's there, if possible."

"That should work."

"But there's one hitch," Avery added. "You have to be wired." The bodyguard handed her a recording device. "Tuck this into your bra and we'll hear every word your uncle says."

They immediately walked outside and climbed into the car. Warren was already waiting for them there, behind the wheel.

"I've done this many times," Avery said, gesturing to the recorder. "Let me help you so it won't fall off."

She reluctantly allowed him to help, since her shoulder was still so sore. The pills didn't seem to be helping much right now. Maybe it was just tension; she wasn't due to take more until six o'clock.

If she was being honest, she was afraid. Nothing had ever frightened her this much before. It was a nerve thing. What had happened to her? The truth of the matter was that a lot had happened to her. She no longer felt like herself.

They carried on until they arrived at the condo building. Warren parked around back, once again to avoid reporters. Warren then spoke to the building's security guard, who allowed them inside.

Soon they were riding up the elevator, the contraption she hated so much. It helped having these guys with her. Still, every squeak or rattle made her pulse quicken.

Once on the tenth floor, Sally walked along the hallway with Avery and Warren right at her heels.

"This is it," she said to the big man beside her when they came to the apartment door.

"Okay, North is in the next apartment, but I'm going to stay right here," Avery explained. He tapped his earpiece. "I'll be able to hear every word that is said. We'll be just a few feet away the whole time."

Sally, full of tension, banged the little knocker several times. In the silence, she stood there, thinking that someone must be home. Her uncle didn't go out these days.

She rapped again, even louder.

Please, I need to get this over with, she thought.

Then the door opened, revealing Anna.

"Oh Sally, I'm so happy to see you," Anna said. "The news told us so little. What a nice surprise to see you out of the hospital! But my goodness, your shoulder is hurt. Is that where you were shot?"

"Yes, that's right. I was lucky, though. You're looking fine, Anna, which is saying a lot considering everything that's going on. Is my uncle in? I need to talk to him."

"Come in, my dear. Your visit saves me a lot of trouble. I was going to come to the hospital today. I think you must have been reading my mind!"

CHAPTER TWENTY-ONE: DECISION TIME

Anna smiled as Sally stepped into the apartment, though it almost seemed as though the housekeeper really was trying to read her mind.

As Sally followed Anna inside, she immediately noticed a terrible odour.

"Anna, what is that smell?" She puckered her nose and tried to keep from heaving. "Has something gone bad?"

"I don't smell anything." Anna sniffed, then shook her head.

"Oh, Anna, it's awful. You must smell it! Something has gone rancid. Will you check the cupboards? It's enough to make a person sick to their stomach." She held her stomach, to demonstrate the point. "Is my uncle in his den?"

"Yes, he is." Anna stopped right in front of her. "You have been a naughty girl, making him so unhappy and causing him all this trouble when he has so much work to do. If you had just gone home, dear, none of this would have happened. Now I have to do something about it."

"I don't understand." Sally frowned, thinking that Anna wore a funny expression. What was the matter with her? The foul smell was overwhelming. It was all she could do, even with her nose pinched, not to heave her stomach. "Never mind, I want to talk to him. While I'm at it, can you get rid of that smell? And make us a cup of tea please?"

"Yes, of course. I have a fresh pot of coffee. Will that do?"

"That would be even better."

Sally had to breathe through her mouth, and it was still awful. As she made her way along the hall, she realized that the odour was worse the closer she got to her uncle's den. How could Anna not smell this?

She took two steps through the open door and didn't need to go any farther. She stood in the doorway, frozen to the spot, not believing the scene before her. Her uncle sat behind his desk, his head lolled back. He had been shot in the chest!

How is this possible? she thought, trying not to throw up her lunch. *I must be seeing things.*

"Anna!" she yelled. When there was no answer, she yelled again. "Anna!"

She forgot all about the wire fastened to her bra and hurried toward the kitchen. She almost bumped into Anna, who was exiting with two cups of coffee on a tray alongside some cookies, which scattered all across the hall floor.

She didn't even look at the mess. "Anna, has someone been here recently?"

At first scream, Avery and Warren had come running into the apartment. They stood at the front of the hall with their guns drawn.

"Sally, look what you made me do! The judge will be very upset!" Anna snapped. "Do you want me to ask him to come to the kitchen? He doesn't like to have coffee in the kitchen. He's very fussy about things like that. Now I'll have to go and clean up this mess!"

"No, we can gather up this stuff later," Sally said slowly, the truth still sinking in. She turned to the two bodyguards. "Avery, Warren, my uncle has been shot. He's in his office, down the hall."

As Warren went to investigate, Avery took Sally and Anna into the kitchen. He kept a firm hand on Anna's shoulder.

"Please, Anna, sit down," Sally said.

She looked up at the sound of the front door banging open. In a moment, North and several other policemen arrived.

Sally pointed toward the den. "In the room down the hall."

They all recognized the smell that was overtaking the apartment. Avery stayed right beside Sally, keeping his eyes on the strange housekeeper who seemed totally unaware of what was going on around her.

CHAPTER TWENTY-ONE: DECISION TIME

Sally walked toward the door that led to the patio and opened it wide to let in some fresh air. She watched as the officers, all in uniform, swarmed through the apartment. She felt stunned, not sure what to do.

It took a few minutes for North to emerge from the den. He sat in the kitchen, across the table from Anna.

"Ma'am," he said to Anna, "did you hear any shots?"

Anna still seemed confused. "No, I didn't."

"Ma'am, the judge has been shot. Do you know who shot him?"

"Shot!" She looked up, startled. "Is he dead?"

"Yes, ma'am. Was there anyone else with you in the apartment before Ms. Cameron arrived?" He waited for her to answer, but she just stared. "Ma'am, you must have seen who shot the judge. Was someone in the office with him?"

Anna honestly looked like she had no idea what he was talking about. There was no way she couldn't have noticed the smell, no matter how she tried to think of an explanation.

"No," she murmured. "He was talking on the phone to Clare. They were very unhappy. So much has gone wrong for us. Everything would have been fine if Sally hadn't spoiled it." Anna turned her angry eyes to Sally. "You wouldn't go home!" She shook her head, looking back to North. "You see, he cheated on me, and that just wasn't fair. He couldn't do that! Especially not with Judith."

"Ma'am," North said, raising his voice. "Did you let someone into the apartment?"

She blinked. "No. There was no one. The judge is fine now. Everything is fine now. Sally's dead. She can't hurt us anymore."

Sally almost jumped up. In that moment, despite the shock and disbelief taking over her mind, she realized the truth about her.

"Look, ma'am, I know it's a shock," North said. "Someone has killed the judge and I have to know who did it."

"Yes, I know, poor man. It was the only way. He was going to leave us and I couldn't let that happen." Anna glanced up, a smile on her lips. "I killed him. Don't you see? We're all right now. Lisa is the crazy one, you know."

North stared at her hard. "When did you shoot Judge Cameron?"

The inspector hesitated, not knowing what to say when Anna didn't answer. They dared not make the same mistakes they had made with Sally's aunt.

"Steve, come here a sec, will you?" North said. A large uniformed cop came into the kitchen. "Read this woman her rights. She's under arrest for murder."

They say there's a thin line between insanity and genius, Sally thought. *Who can say where Anna lies? She's not right in her right mind now, but everything has been too well planned for her to be crazy.*

She wondered if the blackmail pictures had triggered something in Anna's mind.

"Anna, do you want to talk to a lawyer?" North asked.

The housekeeper looked dazed. "No, I have Sally here."

"Damn it, ma'am, she is not your lawyer. Didn't you try to kill her?" North shook his head. This was more than one cop should have to take!

Anna looked across the room toward the patio door, staring at Sally. "She's dead, you know. I did kill her."

Sally couldn't figure out if this was a clever act or if the woman had become deranged.

"Why did you kill her?" North asked, as though speaking to a child.

"Sally betrayed us when she took Lisa away. Everything was all right until she came. I had to kill the girls. They were very

CHAPTER TWENTY-ONE: DECISION TIME

bad girls, getting the judge in trouble. Poor Lisa, she was just too stupid to understand. She was so spoiled all her life and had so much. It was her turn to help us."

North worked to control his temper and kept his voice steady. "Anna, where is the gun you used to kill the judge?"

Suddenly, she perked right up. "It's on the desk where I left it." She looked into his eyes. "The judge was planning to go away with Judith and leave us both. That wasn't nice after we had taken such good care of him. We only wanted what was the best for him. We loved him so much. We always loved him. He was a man who couldn't help the fact that he liked women. You know something? Women liked him, too."

For the next hour, the apartment was busy with policemen, doctors, and investigators coming and going. After some time had passed, a lawyer even arrived to discuss matters with Anna.

"He's supposed to be good," Warren said about the lawyer. "Sally, if this woman had had another chance, she would have killed you."

Sally nodded. "I know that better than anyone. I guess I don't want to believe it. So much was kept secret, so many lives were ruined. But my aunt is a good woman. I wonder, how many times did she close her eyes to the truth?"

Finally, with handcuffs on, Anna was taken out of the apartment and brought to the police station, where she answered questions and faced professional evaluations. North held his temper when she admitted to killing Slipper, although she couldn't even remember Slipper's name.

CHAPTER TWENTY-TWO
ANOTHER DAY, ANOTHER TIME

Avery drove Sally out to Peter's house in the country. After getting out of the car, she sat outside on the lawn waiting for him to come home. Once Peter returned, she filled him in on everything that had happened, although he already knew most of it from talking to North.

She followed Peter to the library, where he immediately began writing his article at the desk. The exclusive story would appear in the paper the following morning.

Peter insisted she take a little holiday until the bandages came off, and of course he wanted her to stay with him. For the next three days, Peter entertained her and her aunt while they regained their strength.

When it came time for Slipper's funeral, Mark flew in on an eight o'clock morning flight from Toronto. To Sally's amusement, North met him at the airport, where they became buddies of sorts. She thought it was because they both had the same job. Even though they worked in different provinces, they followed the same principles.

Sally knew that the main reason for Mark coming out was to make sure that she went home with him. He even bought her a seat on his return flight in the afternoon.

However, she still had a few things that had to be looked after.

CHAPTER TWENTY-TWO: ANOTHER DAY, ANOTHER TIME

* * *

That morning, Sally sat in Peter's kitchen with both Peter and Martha, all of them lost in their own thoughts. They dared not think what was on the others' minds.

They jumped when they heard the peal of the doorbell, but none of them got up. After it had rung a few times, Peter stood and walked to the front of the house, not once looking in Sally's direction.

Martha, too, was hurt that Sally was leaving her brother. As far as she was concerned, they were meant for each other. How many times did real love come along? She didn't think Peter should let it go.

A minute later, Peter appeared in the kitchen with Mark behind them. Sally looked up and smiled at both men.

Mark came forward and leaned down to kiss her gently. "Hi, doll."

"Hi yourself."

Gazing into his face, she remembered the important part he played in her life. Was it possible that she had fallen in love with two men at the same time? The problem was, they were so much alike. But there were differences, too. One of the differences was that Peter made her feel so special. With Mark, she was one of the gang. Which was more important to her?

"Please, sit down and I'll get you a coffee," Martha said.

"Thanks," said Mark. "Wow. The traffic was wild today, and the airport was crazy."

Inside, though, he knew that it was nothing compared to trying to move around Toronto at about four o'clock in the afternoon.

Sally turned to Mark. "Was it a good flight?"

"Not a speck of turbulence." He turned to North. "I hate flying. But then, that's the way it is. I just have to get used to it."

North laughed. "Not afraid of guns or bad guys? Just flying?"

Mark didn't dare think about the tension in the room. He didn't know enough about all the time Sally had spent here, and he didn't want to. All he wanted was to get her on a plane home and everything would be all right. He only too well remembered the kiss he had seen in the hospital.

"Well, Sally, what have you planned for today?" asked Peter.

Why wasn't life like a storybook? Peter wondered to himself. *That way, he would have gotten the girl and it would have been a happy ending.*

The strange thing was that he himself had to head to Toronto soon for a couple of weeks. Maybe he hadn't lost her yet after all.

"I'm going to spend some time with Aunt Lisa," Sally said. "After that, we'll be at the funeral."

She watched as Mark struggled now to show his true feelings. She had to go home, away from everything here, to see where her heart lay. Marriage was a lifetime commitment as far as she was concerned. She had to get it right the first time.

Together, they talked about the loose ends of the case. Anna had been arrested for the murders of Slipper McKinnon, Corey Pearl, Joanna Star, and Hilliard Cameron. She had pleaded guilty the day before in a police interrogation room. Sally had been sitting outside, listening through a speaker.

That poor woman had thought Sally was the cause of all her trouble, but in reality the trouble had been her obligations to the judge. She had loved him for most of the time she had worked for him. Somehow, in her warped mind, she had accepted that she and Lisa shared him. But it had been too much when she found out about his connections to Corey and Joanna. She had killed him out of jealousy.

Tony Clark had been charged for extortion, as it was proven that he had been the photographer behind the blackmail pictures.

CHAPTER TWENTY-TWO: ANOTHER DAY, ANOTHER TIME

His hearing would be coming up in a few months. Even though the pictures had been destroyed, as well as the negatives, North figured that the pictures had already been distributed.

Lisa Cameron had decided to stay right where she was. She rented a space in Sarah's and Blossom's home for a while, until she had decided what to do next. With the judge murdered, she no longer had to worry about getting a divorce. She told Sally that she looked forward to working to help the people living on local reservations.

Sally was pleased that she was leaving her aunt in good hands.

As for her uncle, he was to be cremated. There wasn't even going to be a funeral.

Judith Alves took early retirement and her house went up for sale. She didn't tell anyone where she was planning to go next, except that she intended to leave the country.

Clare was the one to have suffered the most, for she had lost her daughter. When the hours became long and life too quiet, she was plagued by memories that would haunt her for the rest of her life. Sally believed that her aunt was going to help Clare in some way, although she wasn't sure what that meant.

That afternoon, after Slipper's funeral, an airplane took off from the airport's cement runway, taking off smoothly and rising into the sky.

"Why didn't you drive out here?" Mark asked, turning to Sally.

She just laughed and handed him the barf bag from the back of the seat.

OTHER BOOKS BY SHIRLEY

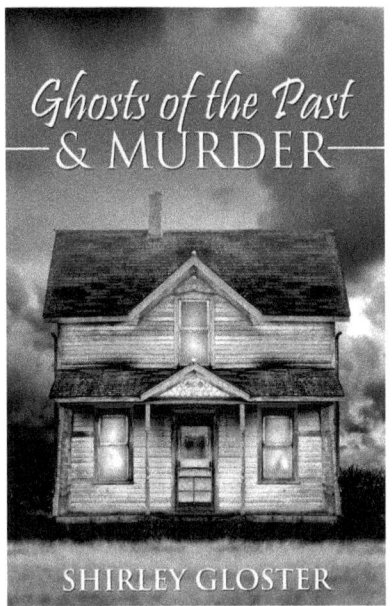

GHOSTS OF THE PAST & MURDER

When newspaper reporter Alex Rutherford receives a tip about a murdered family in the Niagara region, she decides to investigate—especially when she learns that her own family might be involved. Accompanied by her best friend, Ginny, and her dog, Spider, they set out to solve the case.

While hunting for shallow graves in a country cemetery, the investigators meet a handsome police chief and his sidekick from the St. Catharines Police Department. Romance blooms as they join forces to catch the killer.

The mystery deepens as the investigation leads them to an old farmhouse, the disappearances of three men, and a tale of forbidden love that rocks them to the core. Despite getting tangled in these unspeakable crimes, they discover that they'll have no choice but to confront the *Ghosts of the Past*—once and for all.

A HOLIDAY WEEKEND & MURDER

Sally Cameron, a smart and attractive criminal attorney, plans to spend a much-needed holiday weekend with her sister and brother-in-law at their country estate. But when she arrives late Friday evening, she finds many unanswered questions waiting for her.

First, her sister and brother-in-law are missing. Second, she hears a foreboding noise in the night, leaving her to believe someone is up to no good. Third, she discovers a jogging trail behind the house she knew nothing about.

Finally, in desperation, she goes back to the city seeking the help of a dear friend, Detective Joan Troon. Together they return to the estate only to discover an old farmhouse and a mysterious license plate. Soon Sally finds herself entangled in a dangerous police chase and the prisoner of a wanted man.

A NIGHTMARE & MURDER

In this third and final novel in the Sally Cameron series, Sally once again teams up with Inspector Mark Trotter and her friend Joan Troon—not to mention an eye-popping old-friend—as she takes on a new mystery.

Lately, Sally has been haunted by a terrible nightmare, always waking to a scream that never comes out of her mouth. She hears a laugh in the background as a killer reminds her of someone she knows… if only she could remember who it was. The dream seems all too real.

Then the nightmare turns into reality as one by one her friends across the country are mysteriously killed. As she gathers clues—a telephone call, a meeting place on park bench with an old enemy—she is constantly reminded that death is right around the corner.

CPSIA information can be obtained
at www.ICGtesting.com
Printed in the USA
LVHW04s1315300918
591920LV00002B/478/P